Lisa Marie Presley, born in Memphis, Tennessee, U.S. on the 1st of February, 1'
songwriter, the only child of Elvis Presley and Priscilla Presley. During her caree
Lisa Marie released 3 L.Ps: To Whom It May Concern (2003), which went gold in the US, followed by
Now What (2005) then Storm & Grace (2012). She also issued non-album singles, including duets with
Elvis Presley using tracks that were released during his lifetime.

Lisa Marie was born 9 months to the day after her parents' wedding. After they divorced, she lived with
her mum in Los Angeles, with frequent stays with her dad at Graceland in Memphis. Lisa's parents
divorced when she was 4 yrs old. When Elvis passed away on 16th August 1977, nine-yr-old Lisa Marie
became joint heir to his estate with her 59-yr-old grandad, Vernon Presley, and his 87-yr-old mother,
Minnie Mae. After the deaths of Vernon in 1979 then her great-grandma the following year, she became
sole heir, inheriting the estate of c. $100 million on her 25th birthday, 1st Feb. 1993. Lisa Marie sold
85% of her dad's estate during 2004.

A couple of years after the death of Elvis, she attended her 1st rock concert, Queen at The Forum in
Inglewood, California, where she gave Freddie Mercury one of her dad's scarves after the show, while
expressing her liking for theatrics. Priscilla began dating actor Michael Edwards shortly after Elvis passed
away. Lisa Marie was allegedly sexually abused by Edwards when she was a teenager. She told Playboy
magazine in 2003 that Michael would enter her room when drunk then molest her.

Lisa made a video of Don't Cry Daddy as a posthumous duet with her dad during 1997, which was played
on August 16th, 1997, at the tribute concert that marked the 20th anniversary of Elvis Presley's death.
The video used Elvis' original vocal to which new instrumentation & Lisa Marie's vocals were added. She
issued her 1st L.P., To Whom It May Concern, on April 8th, 2003, which hit No. 5 on the Billboard 200
chart, going gold that June 2003.

Lisa wrote all the lyrics except for The Road Between, which was co-written with Gus Black, and co-
wrote every melody. To promote it, she played a concert in the UK. The album's 1st single, Lights Out,
made No. 18 on the Billboard Hot Adult Top 40 chart & UK No. 16. Lisa Marie collaborated with Billy
Corgan on co-written B-side track 'Savior'. In his review of the L.P., Los Angeles Times critic Robert
Hilburn stated that it had a 'a stark, uncompromising tone' and that 'Presley's gutsy, blues-edged voice
has a distinctive flair'.

Pat Benatar performed with Lisa Marie at the VH1 Divas Duets, a concert to benefit the VH1 Save the
Music Foundation held at the MGM Grand Garden Arena on May 22nd, 2003, in Las Vegas. They sang
Pat's hit Heartbreaker, which Presley often performed at her own concerts on tours afterwards. That
year she made a recording of Silent Night for the NBC Holiday Collection, Sounds of the Season.

Lisa Marie's 2nd album, Now What, was released on April 5th, 2005, hitting US No. 9 on the Billboard
200 chart. She co-wrote 10 songs & recorded covers of Don Henley's 'Dirty Laundry', the L.P's first single,
which reached No. 36 on the Billboard 100 AC singles chart, along with the Ramones' 'Here Today and
Gone Tomorrow'. The song 'Idiot' was about some of the men in her life. Now What had a Parental

Advisory sticker. Presley covered Blue Öyster Cult's 'Burnin' for You' as a B-side. Pink made a guest appearance on the track Shine. The video for Dirty Laundry was directed by Patrick Hoelck & the artist George Michael made a cameo appearance in it.

The documentary 'Too Tough to Die: A Tribute to Johnny Ramone' (2006), directed by Mandy Stein, featured Deborah Harry, the Dickies, X, Eddie Vedder, Lisa Marie, and Red Hot Chili Peppers as they staged a benefit concert to celebrate the Ramones' 30th anniversary & raise money for cancer research. Presley appeared in the music video for Johnny Cash's 'God's Gonna Cut You Down' in 2006. Rick Rubin produced the record and Tony Kaye directed the video, which featured a number of celebrities, winning a Grammy Award for Best Short Form Music Video during 2008.

Single 'In the Ghetto' was issued in August 2007, on which Lisa sang a 'duet' with her dad, Elvis having released the original during 1969. The video was put out at the same time as the single, which topped the iTunes sales & made No. 16 on Billboard's Bubbling Under Hot 100 singles chart. The song was recorded to commemorate the 30th anniversary of the death of Elvis. Lisa Marie said that she decided to sing with him, saying "I wanted to use this for something good", shooting the video in New Orleans, with proceeds from the video and single benefiting a new Presley Place Transitional Housing Campus there. Presley appeared on The Oprah Winfrey Show to sing the song with the Harlem Gospel Choir, using vintage footage of her dad.

Lisa Marie joined singer Richard Hawley on stage in London during October 2009, singing vocals on Weary, a song that they'd been working on. Hawley wanted to help Presley relaunch her music career, the pair forming a songwriting partnership in which she wrote the lyrics & he the music. Lisa told Oprah Winfrey that she was recording a new album in London, due for release in 2011.

Her 3rd L.P., Storm & Grace, came out on May 15th, 2012, of which she said: "It's much more of a rootsy record, organic record, than my previous work". It was produced by the Oscar and Grammy winner T Bone Burnett. AllMusic described the record as 'a stronger, more mature & more effective work than one might have expected. Presley is finally developing a musical personality that truly suits her'.

Spinner.com described it as 'the strongest album of her career', while Entertainment Weekly praised the 'smoky, spooky' single You Ain't Seen Nothing Yet. T-Bone Burnett said of collaborating with Lisa Marie on Storm & Grace (2012): "When songs from Lisa Marie Presley showed up at my door, I was curious. I wondered what the daughter of an American revolutionary music artist had to say. What I heard was honest, raw, unaffected and soulful. I thought her father would be proud of her. The more I listened to the songs, the deeper an artist I found her to be. Listening beyond the media static, Lisa Marie Presley is a Southern American folk music artist of great value".

A new compilation of the gospel music of Elvis was issued during 2018, Lisa Marie being incorporated into scenes of her & her dad, along with his vocals, as she sang a duet to the song Where No One Stands Alone.

The Elvis Presley Charitable Foundation (EPCF) was formed by Graceland/Elvis Presley Enterprises, Inc. in 1984 to continue Elvis' tradition of generosity and community service & to honour his memory. The EPCF was overseen by Lisa Marie as chairwoman, and the management team of Graceland/Elvis Presley Enterprises, Inc. Presley Place opened to its first residents during 2001, providing homeless families up to a year of rent-free housing, child day care, career & financial counseling and family management guidance, among other ways of helping them break the cycle of poverty & regain self-esteem and independence.

The Elvis Presley Music Room was also funded by the EPCF, where the kids of Presley Place among others could access musical instruments & instruction and take part in related programs. The EPCF established the Elvis Presley Endowed Scholarship Fund at the College of Communication & Fine Arts at the University of Memphis to assist students majoring in areas of the arts. 'All of us with the EPCF and Elvis Presley Enterprises are extremely proud of this amazing facility. The work that MIFA (the Memphis-based Metropolitan Inter-Faith Association) does truly has an impact on folks' lives & we look forward to this collaboration', stated Lisa Marie.

She joined Oprah Winfrey and her Angel Network & was active in the relief efforts after hurricane Katrina devastated New Orleans and surrounding areas. Presley helped in Memphis, Tennessee. "I'm here, because I definitely needed to do something & it just so happens this is where I'm from. I'm going to do everything I can. People need help—this is a huge catastrophe and everyone needs to stand up".

Her first stop was a food bank, where with the help of FedEx & Kroger, Lisa Marie loaded a truck with groceries then went to Target for toiletries and clothes: "I thought I was going to grab a couple things at the store, but I ended up filling up a truck. I went a little crazy". Her final stop was the Grand Casino Convention Center in Mississippi to distribute the supplies to folk who'd lost everything. One evacuee said, "I really appreciate everything Ms. Presley is doing for us. We have nothing, so we're very grateful for everything that she's doing".

Lisa Marie became a patron of the Dream Factory in 2011, a charity based in Hainault, London, being one of the celebrity guests at the Snowball held at the Prince Regent in Chigwell in aid of the Dream Factory. Actors Ray Winstone & Sid Owen, who were both patrons of the charity, and Amanda Redman were also among guests at the event, which raised $59,000 towards granting the wishes of terminally ill children & those with life-threatening illnesses or disabilities.

Organizer Avril Mills said: "We've granted 83 dreams in under 3 yrs, so the money is going to go towards a lot more dreams. It costs $500 - $5,000 for a dream. Lisa Marie Presley was very nice and she now wants to become a patron of the charity. We talked about the charity & she brought a big framed picture of Elvis, which she got flown over for the Dream Factory from Graceland, and that raised $5,000".

Presley was involved with the Grammy Foundation's Gold Grammy Signature Schools program that recognised leading U.S. public high schools, which made an outstanding commitment to music education during an academic school year. Lisa Marie and music producer Jimmy Jam presented an award to Isaac Hayes at the Memphis Recording Academy Honors on October 22nd, 2005. Many hometown stars attended to watch her, Justin Timberlake, Isaac Hayes & David Porter honored by the Memphis chapter of the Recording Academy.

Presley took part in a Grammy SoundCheck at L.A.'s House of Blues on Nov. 11th, 2005, during which she and other industry professionals met with a group of music students to discuss their career opportunities in the music industry.

Lisa Marie was honoured by the governor of Tennessee, Bill Haslam on June 24th, 2011, who proclaimed a day of recognition for her charitable efforts. A couple of days later she was given a Certificate of Proclamation by the mayor of New Orleans, Mitchell J. Landrieu, in recognition of her dedication & contributions to the city. The proclamation of the City of Memphis on June 28th, 2011, stated:

'Lisa Marie Presley is a humanitarian and philanthropist who continues to focus her efforts on the hometown that she knows & loves, Memphis. Through her efforts and time she's improved homelessness, literacy & raised funds for local charities and organizations. She raises awareness for Memphis & continues to set an example of what one person can do when they put their mind to it. Now, Therefore, I, A.C. Wharton, Jr., Mayor of Memphis, Tennessee, do hereby recognize the lifelong service of this illustrious humanitarian and philanthropist'.

Presley & her family stayed in San Francisco having lived from 2010 - 2016 in a 15th-century manor house in Rotherfield, East Sussex, England, 15 miles east of Saint Hill Manor, the British headquarters of the Church of Scientology. Lisa Marie said during 2013 that she might write an autobiography in the future, stating: "It's not out of the question. I'd like to have my life out there in my own words, rather than speculations". There was a brief look into her personal life in the TV movie, Elvis by the Presleys (2005).

Lisa Marie wed Chicago-born musician Danny Keough on October 3rd, 1988. They had 2 children: a daughter, Riley Keough (born May 29th, 1989), who became an actress and model then a son, Benjamin Storm Keough (October 21st, 1992 – July 12th, 2020). Presley got a quickie divorce in the Dominican Republic on May 6th, 1994. Benjamin died at the age of 27 in Calabasas, California, from a self-inflicted gunshot wound. The Los Angeles County Medical Examiner's Office listed his death as a suicide.

Lisa Marie married artist Michael Jackson on May 26th, 1994, 20 days after her divorce from Danny, whose younger brother Thomas Keough was an official witness at their wedding. The couple had first met in 1975 when the 7-yr-old Presley attended several of his concerts in Las Vegas. A friend of hers said, "their adult friendship began during November 1992 in L.A".

When child molestation accusations against Jackson became public he became dependent on Lisa Marie for emotional support, who was concerned about his faltering health & his prescription drug addiction. Presley said, "I believed he didn't do anything wrong, and that he was wrongly accused & yes, I started falling for him. I wanted to save him. I felt that I could do it". Soon afterwards she persuaded Michael to settle the allegations out of court and go into rehabilitation to recover.

Lisa Marie appeared in Jackson's 'You Are Not Alone' video directed by Wayne Isham, in June 1995 but the following January she filed for divorce citing irreconcilable differences. Michael's make-up artist, Karen Faye, later said that he'd planned to file for divorce first but had relented after Presley pleaded with him not to then found out the following day that she'd done so herself.

Lisa Marie told Oprah Winfrey during October 2010 that she & Jackson had tried to reconcile for 4 yrs following their divorce and that she'd traveled the world to be with him. After his death the previous year, Presley had 'felt shattered'. She got engaged to musician John Oszajca in November 1998 but broke it off after meeting Nicolas Cage at a party, who she wed on August 10th, 2002. Cage filed for divorce on November 25th that year, which was finalized during 2004.

Danny Keough was a bass guitar player in her band in 2005, having been her musical mentor, Presley still regarding him as a close friend who lived in the guest house of her home. She said of her relationship with Danny after they separated: "I don't know how, but we've managed to stay close... There's others that I have pain or betrayal associated with that I won't have anything to do with, but he & I had a special thing. Unconditional". Following rumours that she and Keough were planning to remarry, Lisa Marie said during 2003: "Danny is my best friend, always has been, always will be. I love him unconditionally, but we're not together. It's not like that". Keough & Presley became closer again after she divorced Michael Jackson.

Lisa Marie married for a 4th time on January 22nd, 2006, to Michael Lockwood, her guitarist, music producer, and director. Danny was the best man at the wedding, held in Japan. Presley revealed in March 2008 that she was pregnant. Lockwood became a dad for the 1st time on October 7th that year when Lisa Marie gave birth to fraternal twin girls, Harper Vivienne Ann Lockwood & Finley Aaron Love Lockwood, by Caesarean section at Los Robles Hospital & Medical Center in Thousand Oaks, California.

Presley filed for divorce from Michael during 2016. The couple's kids were placed in the temporary care of Priscilla Presley in February the following year after Lisa Marie alleged in a divorce court filing challenging Lockwood's request for spousal support that there were inappropriate images of their children on his personal computer. The Beverly Hills Police Department investigated the allegations, examining over 80 electronic devices, but found no criminal activity, referring the matter to investigators in Tennessee. The Tennessee Bureau of Investigations closed its investigation of the allegations made by Presley in 2017, stating that there was no evidence of a crime. The divorce was finalized during 2021.

Lisa Marie, along with her friend, fellow Memphian and Scientologist Isaac Hayes, opened the Literacy, Education & Ability Program (LEAP) in October 1997. LEAP is run by Applied Scholastics, a group run by Scientologists.

Presley received the Humanitarian Award from the Church of Scientology-supported World Literacy Crusade on January 5th, 2002, for her efforts to help U.S. children learn study skills. She was given her award by Isaac Hayes, Chaka Khan, and Yolanda King, daughter of Martin Luther King Jr. World Literacy Crusade is considered by its critics to be a front group for the Church of Scientology. Lisa Marie addressed a U.S. Congressional hearing on September 26th that year, in opposition to the use of medication in treating ADHD, stating:

"I've spoken to children who've been forced to take a cocaine-like stimulant to control their behavior; I've shared their sense of sheer desperation. Children have been wrenched from their family's care simply because their parents favoured an alternative, drug-free approach to addressing educational & behavioral problems. The psychotropic drugging of millions of children has to stop".

Addressing the committee as the International Spokesperson for Children's Rights, for the Citizens Commission on Human Rights (CCHR), a group run by Scientologists, Presley stated that parents should be informed about alternatives to drugs so that they may "make an informed choice about their child's educational and medical needs". Lisa Marie left Scientology during 2014, although she'd been getting increasingly unhappy with the organization from 2008.

After Elvis Presley's death at Graceland on August 16th, 1977, his will appointed his dad, Vernon Presley, as executor & trustee. The beneficiaries of the trust were Vernon, Elvis' grandma Minnie Mae Presley, and Lisa Marie, whose inheritance was to be held in trust until her 25th birthday. Following Vernon's death in 1979, Elvis' ex-wife Priscilla was named as one of 3 trustees in his will; the others were the National Bank of Commerce in Memphis & Joseph Hanks, who'd been the family's accountant.

Lisa Marie became the only surviving beneficiary when Minnie Mae Presley passed away during 1980. She inherited her dad's estate on her 25th birthday in 1993, estimated at $100 million. Lisa Marie became more closely involved in the management of the Elvis Presley Trust and its business entity, Elvis Presley Enterprises, Inc. during 1998, becoming its owner & chairman of the board until February 2005, when she sold 85% of the estate's business holdings to CKX, Inc., excluding Graceland and the property within it.

Lisa Marie opened a new exhibit, 'Elvis ... Through His Daughter's Eyes', in February 2012, which was included in the Graceland VIP Tour, featuring 200 items assembled by Presley & the Graceland Archives staff. The personal exhibit revealed Lisa Marie's experience of growing up with Elvis, home movies, toys, and rarely seen family mementos being among the items on display.

Elvis named one of his private aircraft, a converted Convair 880 jet, after her in November 1975, having spent over $1 million refurbishing it to use as his main transport while on tour. The Lisa Marie & 1 of his other planes, Hound Dog II, were displayed at Graceland, both planes being put up for sale during January 2015, but they were still exhibited there 7 yrs later.

Lisa Marie had a heart attack at her home in Calabasas, California, on January 12th, 2023. Her heart was restarted by CPR en route to a Los Angeles hospital, but she passed away later that day at the age of 54. News of her death was released by Priscilla Presley. Many celebrities including Leah Remini and John Travolta paid tribute to her on social media & made public statements. Lisa Marie's last public appearance was a couple of days earlier, at the 80th Golden Globe Awards, which she attended with her mum. Presley was buried in Graceland with Elvis and son Benjamin.

Discography

Studio albums

Title	Details	Peak chart positions					Certifications
		US	AUS	GER	SWI	UK	
To Whom It May Concern	Release date: Apr. 8th, 2003 Label: Capitol Records Formats: CD, music download	5	54	74	86	52	RIAA: Gold
Now What	Release date: April 5th, 2005 Label: Capitol Records Formats: CD, music download	9	—	—	76	—	
Storm & Grace	Release date: May 15th, 2012 Label: Universal Republic Formats: CD, vinyl, music download	45	—	—	—	—	

Singles

List of singles, with selected chart positions, showing year released and album name

Title	Year	Peak chart positions						Album
		US AC	US Adult	US Pop	AUS	NZ	UK	
Lights Out	2003	—	18	34	29	28	16	To Whom It May Concern
Sinking In		—	—	—	—	—	—	
Dirty Laundry	2005	36	—	—	—	—	—	Now What
Idiot		—	—	—	—	—	—	

Thanx		—	—	—	—	—	—
In the Ghetto (with Elvis Presley)	2007	—	—	—	—	—	—	Non-album single
You Ain't Seen Nothing Yet	2012	—	—	—	—	—	—	Storm & Grace
I Love You Because (with Elvis Presley)	—		—	—	—	—	—	Non-album single
Over Me	2013	—	—	—	—	—	—	Storm & Grace

— denotes a single that didn't chart or wasn't released in that territory.

Tours

S.O.B. Tour (2003–2004)

Now What Tour (2005–2006)

Storm & Grace Tour (2012–2014)

Further reading

Taraborrelli, J. Randy (2004). The Magic and the Madness. Terra Alta, WV: Headline. ISBN 0-330-42005-4.

Finstad, Suzanne (2006). Child Bride: The Untold Story of Priscilla Beaulieu Presley. Terra Alta, WV: Headline. ISBN 978-0-307-33695-8.

Lisa Marie Presley was the real deal, her CD, 'Now What', being a strong collection of well crafted, emotionally charged songs that showcased her distinctive smoky voice & displayed her artistic vision. Opening with the infectious 'I'll Figure It Out', the L.P. explored naked emotions and intoxicating moods, standouts tracks including her incendiary cover of Don Henley's 'Dirty Laundry', the naughty punk rave up, 'Idiot', featuring Steve Jones of The Sex Pistols on guitar, & the elegiac ballad, Now What. Lisa Marie put up a great big middle finger to her detractors on her album, doing it her way. Raw and real, Now What showed what an impassioned, confident artist she was, not afraid of letting folk into her own dark world.

What was the 1st music that'd affected Presley?

'I grew up during the '70s, so that music is my favourite. A lot of singer-songwriters were having success back then & being played on the radio. That's the time period of music that really had an influence on me. The music that had the most profound affect on me was Pink Floyd's The Wall. From age 13 until now, that never dies'.

Had the alienation in the lyrics of that record connected with Lisa Marie as a teenager?

'Aye, completely, I was completely there. That L.P. spoke for me like nothing else. The whole entirety of it too. I loved it. I liked 'Hey You', 'Mother', 'Comfortably Numb', all those songs. I loved that. It was recorded back then but it still stands the test of time. It's still so powerful. It's one of those albums that never dies'.

The lyrics on Presley's latest L.P. were very strong and expressive. What lyricists had most impact on her?

'I'm a huge fan of Roger Waters lyric writing. Definitely the lyrics on The Wall & Dark Side (Of The Moon)'.

Roger Waters hadn't been afraid to go to a dark place and Lisa Marie wasn't either...

'He was both literal & metaphorical. That was a huge influence on me when I think about it. Roger Waters' writing really got to me. 'Brain Damage', all those kinds of songs, 'and if the band you're in starts playing different tunes I'll see you on the dark side of the moon'. Things like that just got me. That's the only kind of music that really affected me, impacted me. I like honest, dark music that's saying something. That's your job as a writer. Music is some sort of communication. That's the music I respond to & that's the music that I write. The only subject that I was good at in school was writing. I used to be a serious writer growing up. I wrote poems, short stories. That's when I'd be the happiest, when I could write. That was obvious at a young age'.

Did Presley have to be unhappy to write?

'No I don't, I think that's a misconception. I think you can go to the necessary place to purge something that's on your mind. I don't think that an artist has to live a dark life to paint a dark picture, to write a dark song. That's a misconception that people fall into that you're angry or dark or this or that. I say, 'No, this is what I felt about the subject at the time. I'm trying to capsulize it and make it universal for other folk.

I think folk thought that I was dark & moody for the first record. The irony of the whole thing is that when I write all of these songs then I really tackle it, look at it dead on, put it in a song and give it life in a song, it resolves the whole thing for me. 'Shine' from the new album is a really good example of that. I'm saying a lot without saying a lot. A lot of these songs on the L.P. are about me tackling the subject of, 'I'm kind of an outsider, I'm not really part of anything. I'm not part of a clique, I'm not part of a pop culture. I'm not part of what people thought I should be before I was born or during or whatever'. You name it. I'm not really part of any of that nor do I wanna be. There's been times when I've been angry at that or when I've tried really hard. 'Now What' is a vulnerable take on having tried and feeling like I failed'.

At what?

'At being something that I wasn't or trying to do something that I was told I should do but it didn't work out for me'.

'Now What' had a skeletal, Pink Floyd feel.

'That song was about me having an anchor in my life & trying to be what everyone else was being. Then I tried it but I didn't cut it. I disagreed with it. Then I felt like the outcast'.

Folk wanting Lisa Marie to conform?

'Yes, to something, to an idea, to something. It's very general, the subject matter could apply to anything, but for me personally I'm giving you an overview about trying to be a part of something that I really thought was the right thing for me to do but I didn't do good at it. Maybe I compromised a little bit, did something under pressure or tried to do something that everyone was doing and were looked up to doing, but I couldn't do it. It's like, you were there but now you're not, so what am I going do now? 'Shine' is kind of the same thing on that subject but it's a more uplifting take on it, like, 'Look, it's fine. I'm okay at being what I am. I'm not beating myself up anymore for not following what everybody is doing or what I'm supposed to be doing''.

'Turbulence' had very pointed lyrics. Was it cathartic for Presley to write that song?

'A lot of folk around me like that song, because they know who I wrote it about. It was one of those songs where I really nailed somebody, I really needed to get that out of my system. While I was on the road I kept writing lyrics, because there was this particular person who'd really raked me over the coals. I'm pretty good with having a bullsh*t detector & spotting where people are coming from, but this one slipped through the cracks a bit. I needed to get that out'.

While promoting her 1st record Lisa Marie was part of the Wango Tango Festival show at the Rose Bowl, performing in front of over 90,000 fans.

'It was terrifying. That's not my format, playing with a lot of pop acts. I went out there with some really dark songs, which wasn't the deal there. I shouldn't have been there'.

From being a very private person to putting herself in the spotlight in front of all those folk must've been difficult.

'I don't think I really realized what I was getting into on that front. It was backwards for me. I had no real experience performing live, so I had to find my way by doing things like that over and over again. It was a bit messy & thankfully I have different management now, so that's not going to happen. I won't compromise, throwing myself into a situation that I can't handle anymore. I did take them on, because I figured that if I have to prove myself then I've got to get used to it. That was kind of my attitude, you're going to just have to do it and deal with it'.

That courage, that strong sense of self, where did Presley think that came from?

I think that Scientology has a lot to do with that. The fact that it's a self-discovery. I've been doing it since I was 19. I was introduced to it when I was 10. That's what I was doing in my 20s & a lot of my 30s was making progress there in that religion'.

Taking control of her life?

'Yes. Getting rid of things that aren't so great & becoming more myself in doing that'.

Knowing the pressure, unfair comparisons and high expectations that'd be placed on Lisa Marie's pursuit of a musical career, had that made it a tougher choice?

'I think I naively went about writing. My main focus was 'I'm going to try to break through this regardless, try to get my own fans & hopefully allow my music to affect others like it's done for me in my life'. I've got a strong fan base and I've gotten really great responses. I think I was really naïve at the beginning, I didn't know what mountain I was climbing, because it is unfair & folk do want to see you fail and they're overly critical.

This album has been basically well received but there were a couple of personal shots taken at me by critics. That's the thing. It has nothing to do with the music. You can tell that they have this preconceived idea of me. Even if there's a compliment, they'd had to make some personal jab. It wasn't even about the music, it was about something else that they already had in mind about me from my other career in the tabloids'.

How did Lisa Marie get beyond it?

'It's one of those things where I like to say the phrase 'spitting against the tidal wave', because that really explains what it feels like. Honestly I think it's the fans writing me and the letters that I get & when I meet them. I was doing an autograph signing in Canada the other day and this girl burst into tears when she met me & she said, "My father was murdered when your first record came out and your record got me through it". I completely lost it. I thought, 'This is why I make music'.

I think making that kind of difference with my music on a positive level is my ultimate goal. It scares me if my records are going well. I noticed that some folk didn't like it when the 1st record did well, so they started coming after me. Campaigns were out on me later, completely trying to shoot me down, because they didn't like the fact that the record did good. That side of things is a sort of nature of the beast. Before that I think I dealt with it pretty well. That wasn't happening so much. I think when there's success they start to target you. I'm almost afraid for this record to do well, because then what's gonna happen?'

What was the first rock show that Presley saw?

'Probably Queen. I think I saw them in 1978 or 1979 at The Forum. I remember bringing Freddie Mercury a scarf of my Dad's, which I gave to him after the show. I loved it. I loved the theatrics. I loved Freddie. I thought Queen were awesome. I'm a big fan of theatrics, like Marilyn Manson's live show. I've seen him 8 times now'.

What about KISS?

'I never saw them live but I liked them when I was younger. We played on the same bill at the Wango Tango Festival but I didn't see them play later. I wanted to get out of there when I was done. I did what I had to do then I ran out of there'.

In the book, Elvis By the Presleys, Lisa Marie spoke about one of her favourite records growing up being Sweet Inspiration by The Sweet Inspirations, the female singing group that used to perform with Elvis. What was it about their music that appealed to her?

'I loved the song Sweet Inspiration. They were like The Supremes then but they weren't as high profile. I think they were underrated, because my father snagged them at some point. Soulful music always impacted me. Gospel music. I just loved their voices and that song. I think I had a little 45, which I played all the time'.

David Cassidy said that she visited the set of The Partridge Family TV show. Elvis called the set to speak to David who hung up on him a few times, because he didn't believe that it was actually him.

'I was a huge fan of The Partridge Family. I was also a huge fan of The Jeffersons, Good Times, Sanford & Son, all those TV shows from back then but I did like The Partridge Family and I did go to the set. They were in the middle of taping. I was probably 3 or 4 yrs old, I was told & I kind of have a recollection that I was comfortable enough with the show and comfortable enough with them & felt connected enough with them that I was sitting in my Mum's lap, then I got up out of her lap and ran onto the stage while they were taping & I jumped into Shirley Jones' lap.

They had to stop the taping. I didn't think they knew who I was yet. They just knew this little girl had run up then landed in Shirley Jones' lap. I liked 'I Think I Love You'. That record has got me singing that on 'Raven'. On the intro on 'Raven', the 3-yr old voice is me singing 'I Think I Love You'. You hear my mum saying, "Sing it right" and I just thought that was funny. The 'ba-ba-ba-ba' in the beginning is the intro for 'I Think I Love You'.

My mum would always tape me singing then send it off to my dad when he was on tour, so she'd have me singing songs into a tape recorder & she had that. She was getting mad at me and I was sort of pouting then the song plays. At the end she's telling me to sing a line that I know is wrong, so I'm arguing with her, I keep repeating, "No, it's not that. It's 'I've got so much to think about, I don't know what I'm up against'". I kept doing that then I sang, "I Think I Love You" at the end'.

Presley had said, "All true artists are natural rebels". That sense of rebellion began with Elvis then worked its way through the Rolling Stones to the punk rock scene to others that ran against the tide. She seemed to connect with that rebel instinct.

'Yes, I'm carrying the torch but it's in my own way. It's like what I said in my liner notes to my parents. We've all pioneered different roads. He had a huge road during the '50s, it was very conservative & he shook everything up. That was a cross to bear, having pissed a lot of folk off but made a lot of people happy all at the same time. My mum has her own thing where she was a very young girl who was presented with an opportunity where I don't think many women have crossed or walked. Me, I am who I am and I'm doing my own music in my own way & developing my own fan base, going against what people probably think I should do and what I should or shouldn't be'.

Lisa Marie was taking the road less travelled.

'Exactly, so that's my thing. That's the sort of burden & cross that I bear. Then there's the crucifixion part, where 'You're not this or you're not that'. One of the critics was giving me a compliment but was upset that I did a Ramones cover on the new L.P., not an Elvis song. You know that's going on'.

Why had punk rock connected with Presley so strongly?

'The punk rock bands were the most committed with what they were doing. That was so attractive to me back then. I liked the Sex Pistols, The Clash. I wasn't that familiar with The Ramones until I made friends with Johnny Ramone, believe it or not. I got a lot of lecturing, he made me watch Rock And Roll High School & listen to The Ramones compilation CDs after we met. I dug it a lot. It's a shame. When the Ramones were out there they didn't get played, they never got a gold record.

Even when I got on the cover of Rolling Stone, Johnny said, "You got on the cover of what?" he started bitching at me, "20 yrs I was in the Ramones and we never got on the cover of Rolling Stone". That's the part that I relate to even more now. I didn't make a record of pop music & I didn't do a record of Elvis covers and I didn't superimpose my voice in with his, which is what a lot of folk wanted me to do'.

'Here Today, Gone Tomorrow' by the Ramones was a hidden bonus track on Lisa Marie's latest CD.

'Johnny picked that song. He told me that he wanted me to do that song for the Ramones covers album. It didn't work out timing wise. That would've come out before my 1st record. All I did last summer was write, make the record & visit the hospital or go to his house. That's how I spent my time up until the day he died'.

Was Johnny proud of Presley?

'He was true punk but he was like a father figure to me. He got very paternal with me and there were a couple of times like when I was married to Nic that he'd say, "You used to be so low profile & I used to think that was really cool, what the f*ck are you doing being all over the place? At all the premieres, you're getting photographed all the time, what are you doing? That's not cool. What you were doing before was cool". I said 'I can't help it that I'm with this person who has to make appearances and I'm with him'.

He picked 'Here Today, Gone Tomorrow', because he thought it'd be good for my voice but I thought he was crazy. He'd always scare me by saying "Ramones songs sound easy but they're not easy". He made me freak out. I remember sitting with him in his living room when I told him that I was going to do this cover. His eyes lit up then he got this little mischievous twinkle that he was getting quite often towards the end there, only I brought it out or his wife, which was really funny.

He got that little twinkle turn on then he looked at me & I said, "Okay, I'm gonna do it. I'm promising you now that it's gonna go on the record". Then I called Johnny to tell him that I really wanted him to play on it. He said, "I will if I can sit down", but the day we did the track was the day that he died. I was supposed to go to see him that morning, because they were laying down the track and I had to listen then I got the call'.

Lisa Marie got Steve Jones of The Sex Pistols to play on it.

'Right. I was petrified to ask him. You want to talk about serious punk musos. Johnny wasn't so thrilled about my first record. He liked '50s - '60s music, that was it & my dad. It was too complicated and there was too much going on for him. He didn't like it. I played him 'I'll Figure It Out' 1st then he lit up. He said, "Wow, this a lot better, this is really good". It was the first time that he gave me a compliment, I was like, "Wow!"'

The intro was reminiscent of The Cure.

'Yeah, I'm a big Cure fan too. So then I wanted Steve Jones to play on 'Idiot'. I was trying to be all cool & write a song that didn't have a chorus, because I thought of honoring 'I Wanna Be Sedated', which kind of just starts off with what is the chorus. I had 'Idiot' but it had no chorus. Linda Perry came to write the chords then she left and I wrote the lyrics. I played it for those two, Johnny & Steve. I told Steve that I wanted him to play on it.

Those punk divas were sitting there and they were no bullsh*t when it came to music. Johnny liked it but he looks at me then goes, "Lisa, you don't have a chorus. What the f*ck are you doing not writing a chorus?" I'm thinking 'I'm being all cool and trying to make it all punk with no chorus'. He rips into me then I go, "Okay, okay". I start laughing. Steve told me that he'd take it with him to see if he'd come up with some ideas. The next day I called Linda Perry back to say, "We need to write a chorus", so she came then we sat with an acoustic guitar & she just wrote the chords with me, left again then I wrote the lyrics'.

What instruments did Presley play?

'I don't play any really. I kind of dabble around. I used to play drums. I can play a little guitar but I don't know what I'm doing. I go off of feel, I don't go off of actual chords. Anytime anyone tries to teach me I go brain dead. I used to play piano, so I can dilly-dally around but it's nothing serious'.

Lisa Marie made a video back in '97, shown at an Elvis Tribute concert in Memphis, when she sang a duet with Elvis on 'Don't Cry Daddy'. How had that come about?

'I did that because I was tired of being some figure that just came out, smiled, waved then left. I was asked to appear at the tribute concert. I said I'd come. I had this whole vision on this airplane. I think I was flying from New York to Florida, oddly enough I was in the bathroom when I had this whole vision. I was going to call David Foster and I knew the song. I was on the plane when I was thinking about it then I started getting emotional with of the idea.

I definitely had that relationship with my dad where I felt a lot of pain & I knew that song would be very meaningful. I loved the song. I called David Foster to tell him that he needed to produce this thing for me, that it was only a one-time deal. I'm not selling out but I just wanted to do something for the fans. That night was something special. David said he'd do it. That was kind of the beginning of the whole deal. It was only done for the fans for that one night. Believe me, that could've been packaged then sold. It turned out pretty well I thought'.

What was in Presley's record collection?

'It's always playlists. It's everything from the Bee Gees to Marilyn Manson to Heart to Jim Croce to Gordon Lightfoot to John Denver to Pink Floyd to Aretha Franklin to The O'Jays to Teddy Pendergrass. It's all over the place. I always had diverse taste'.

Music had become much more compartmentalized since the '70s. There was much less diversity on the airwaves.

'It's like Stepfordville right now. I think the big revolution is going to be satellite, because they play no adverts and they're all over the place stylistically. That's what I listen to, I listen to the '70s station. It's funny now 'cos I was just thinking about this big market now of folk wearing old concert T-shirts; Cheap Trick, Pink Floyd, this one, that one & everyone is sort of missing this time period where it was normal to hear a variety of music on the radio, this emotional music, this meaningful music.

Music made by singer songwriters getting into the charts. I was shocked that I even landed in the top 10 with my new CD. I couldn't believe it. I immediately thought that this is a female rock record and there's no place for it right now. I really had no expectations & I was shocked that it landed in there. I was really happy about it but then I thought 'I landed at 9 but I landed at 5 with my first L.P., so the critics are gonna think, "Oh it didn't do as well"', but 1st of all, the charts and the music sales & all of that is different now than it was with the first record. Also the 1st record had a lot more radio support.

We have no radio backup right now. They're not really spinning the single. We've mostly had a TV campaign, because we knew that we weren't going to have radio, which is only now slowly adding it. There was a lot of support for 'Lights Out', the 1st single on the first record but they kept playing it on pop radio, which isn't my venue, it isn't my place. It was shocking to me to make it into the top 10, because this is an uncompromised record.

Melissa Etheridge and I were bitching about it. She met me for Interview magazine when she said, "Folk keep asking me, 'When are you going to put out another record? because the last single that anybody played of hers was 'Come To My Window' and she's put out 5 records since then'. There's just a lot of craziness going on & I really didn't think I had a shot. I had a couple of melt downs before thinking that I was spitting against a tidal wave. I knew about the pressure of the sophomore jinx and the curiosity factor & it's all nerve wracking. In the end I hoped that the music would stand out and speak for itself'.

When had Lisa Marie realised that she had a good voice?

'I don't know that I even have a good voice to be honest with you. What I can do is I can emote really well. My voice has got its own thing, it's either gonna hit you right or it's not gonna hit you right. I have an ability to emote but it's not necessarily technically a good voice. I realized that I could do that, be emotional, use my voice to deliver my emotions in whichever way I needed to. I probably just realized that when I did a cover of 'Baby, I Love You' by Aretha Franklin when I was 21 yrs old. I was really into that. I was black on that one. It never came out. I was just seeing if I could sing, so I went in & covered that one, which isn't easy then I thought, "Okay, some people thought it was black when they heard it and that's a really good sign"'.

Did Presley sing in front of a mirror when growing up?

'Always. I always had a tennis racket, which I used as a guitar & I'd have some kind of crazy microphone whether it'd be a bottle of lotion or whatever the hell I could grab. I was doing that from 2 or 3 yrs old but I sort of suppressed my interest in singing. I'd sort of dabble, go take voice lessons and just do scales, which I don't think did anything for me. I feel more comfortable singing live now. I'm much better at singing in public than speaking in public, like at the Grammys. That flipped me right the f*ck out. I thought 'Why am I here?' I can't talk at the podium. I find singing more comforting'.

Did Lisa Marie regard Now What as a success in that she'd created a record of no compromise or did she judge it in commercial terms or how it affected listeners?

'For me, it's the letters I received & the response that I got from fans inspired me to make a 2nd record. I thought that if I was affecting these people's lives then I'd continue, and it's worth a month of having my ass out in the press when the record comes out & all the critics. For me to be able to do that in the end is sort of what I focus on and my other thing was that as long as this record is better & as long as I'm growing, I'll continue produce music.

A long time ago when Robert Hilburn was interviewing me I asked him, "Do you think they're gonna rip me apart?" He said, "Not long ago folk used to have a career. They put out a few records then one breaks". You don't really have that now. The attention span of the industry is that of a lizard. It's like box office. It depends on how much it makes then it's out of everybody's mind. It's like with U2. They had records before they broke huge. It's not like that anymore.

All I can hope for in the writing and recording of these records is that I'm building a fan base. Each time I'm getting better, I'm not getting worse. I want to feel like I'm growing & getting better all the time. I'd rather have a career like Radiohead. They have a strong fan base and they occasionally get played on the radio but mostly they have a lot of fans & they kind of quietly go about their business doing their thing'.

Presley's first single was a cover of Don Henley's 'Dirty Laundry'. Did she think that the tabloid mentality had become worse than when Henley's song came out during the '80s?

'Yeah, It's a bloodbath now. It's a f*cking bloodbath. It's so bad, eg. my record comes out then lands in the top 10, it's all good everything's good. I went to the in-store CD signing for the record, showed up in a gas station attendant outfit. All that was covered by magazines like US Weekly was rip on the fact that I wore a gas station attendant outfit to this thing. That's all they paid attention to. That's just a stupid minor little example of where we're at.

The record comes out, it's a good record, it lands in the top ten. No, none of that. It's a good thing that female rock record got into the top 10. Again, none of that. I chose to record 'Dirty Laundry', because that's the nature of the way things are right now. It's not just even my own personal life, it's just anybody's and the irony is doing all this press in the U.S. It was really refreshing to go to Canada, because they're so into the music. They're not as sensationalistic, I was shocked.

When I was there doing all the interviews & I was explaining 'Dirty Laundry', they agreed with what I was talking about. It's the shows we watch, it's what we focus on, people being celebrities for no good reason right now. We're focusing on these pretty Barbies and whether they're fat or thin or tan or who they're with. It's kind of the way things are then the irony is that they use something I said that's more on the sensationalistic side & use that as the story'.

Which songs did Lisa Marie wish that she'd written?

'I'd say 'Lover You Should Have Come Over' by Jeff Buckley. I'm a huge Buckley fan. I never saw him live but I saw the DVD. I love that song. Oddly enough, 'Shadowboxer' by Fiona Apple, that's one I f*ckin' love. The Bee Gees were amazing, God those boys are talented. Still to this day if anyone breaks out any of their songs I go crazy. Everyone goes crazy. I also like Gordon Lightfoot's 'If You Could Read My Mind' or there's one John Denver song that just kills me'.

Presley and her mum picked the songs for the Elvis By the Presleys CD. Which Elvis songs meant most to her?

'I love 'How Great Thou Art', because that's what I was around for. I like the earlier stuff too. I was around to watch him record it & went to all the shows in the '70s. There's a song called 'It's Over' that killed me. There's a song called 'Mary In the Morning' that I just love. There's some obscure ones that were never singles. Separate Ways wasn't paid nearly enough attention to as it should've been. It's really beautiful. I like 'Just Pretend', that killed me. I also love 'You Gave Me A Mountain' too'.

Lisa Marie Presley inherited her dad's eyes, lips and fame, being known across the world as the only child of the King of Rock 'n' Roll & wife, Priscilla, who said that Elvis "looked petrified" the 1st time that he held her, but was soon buying Lisa expensive jewelry, a miniature fur coat and flying to Utah with her so that she could see snow for the 1st time. Priscilla stated that he gave her everything a child "shouldn't have and couldn't appreciate".

Elvis didn't like making love to a woman who'd given birth, Lisa Marie's arrival leading to sexual estrangement between them, so before long they were both were having affairs, divorcing 5 yrs later. Although Lisa was mainly brought up by Priscilla, she spent a lot of time at Graceland with Elvis, having been there when he passed away on August 16th, 1977. When he was found on the bathroom floor, she watched as people tried to revive him, asking, "What's wrong with my daddy? Something's wrong with my daddy & I'm going to find out".

Elvis' death deepened they mystery surrounding his daughter--People magazine dubbing Lisa Marie "the most carefully secluded of all celebrity children". During her seclusion she went through a druggy phase, taking sedatives, marijuana and cocaine, which she said ended after she embraced Scientology. When Lisa was 20, she got pregnant then wed Danny Keough, an unknown musician. They had a couple of kids, Danielle Riley then Benjamin Storm.

Their marriage lasted for 6 years, until she left Danny for Michael Jackson during 1994, marrying him in the Dominican Republic in a ceremony that even Priscilla didn't know about. There was widespread skepticism about any physical union, as Jackson had just faced civil charges of sexually abusing a 13-yr-old boy. On their 1st anniversary, Diane Sawyer asked the couple if they'd had sex, Lisa Marie indignantly responding, "Yes, yes, yes!" but 7 months later she filed for divorce, her lawyer declaring that the marriage was "a mistake, everyone knows".

She then met longtime Elvis aficionado, actor Nicolas Cage at a party in 2001 when they began a relationship, broke up then got back together a couple of times, before getting hitched in Hawaii but he filed for divorce 107 days later. On her 1st L.P., To Whom It May Concern, she sounded like a pissed off Sheryl Crow, as her southern-fried rock rumbled with accusations, apologies, sarcasm & cursing. Most artists made records for money or attention. Lisa didn't need the money.

'I didn't do it to get attention. I hate attention. When I have to speak in public, I get so neurotic that I lose control of my tongue, my legs, and whatever else. If I'm standing in front of a lot of folk, I feel that they're thinking about me, their speculation, but I want to be heard. I've been writing & recording songs since I was 20, for cathartic reasons, as an outlet. I just haven't been doing it publicly'.

Presley had signed her record contract over 4 yrs earlier. Why had it taken so long to make an album?

'Honestly, I just needed to find my way, stylistically. I was anal about the final production. I didn't want to learn the ropes publicly; I couldn't afford that. I knew that there was going to be more attention on me that anyone else putting out a debut record. If I wanted to be a novelty, I could've easily called a top writer then turned into a pop star. I could've done that years ago, but I wanted to be looked at as an artist, so I couldn't do anything stupid or shallow or silly'.

Was Lisa Marie writing silly songs?

'I never had a fluff problem. It was always the opposite: "Let's get you to lighten up and put some more radio-friendly stuff out there". My songs were pretty dark, haunting'.

There were a dozen songs, including a bonus track. How many of them were happy?

'I was talking with Nic Cage last night, who lectured me: "I told you, you should put a happy song on the record". I said, "f*ck that! I'm not doing it". Music that's happy doesn't move me, so the answer to the question is 'None''.

Presley had rarely talked to the press before. If she didn't have a record to promote, would she still be talking to them?

'No. What else would I talk about? My upbringing? I don't like talking about myself. At this point I'm thinking, 'What've I done?' The hard part is opening up for the 1st time. I have to combat 30 yrs of speculation & tabloid stuff. I have to go out there saying, "Hi, I'm not that person". However, I understand the curiosity, and I don't want to be a c*nt or look like I'm hiding something. I realize why I feel vulnerable & afraid--a lot of people do interviews based on what their publicists tell them. I put my ass out there, cellulite and all. I can be very unfiltered & unedited, which might kick me in the ass one day. I'm being really honest, and if I get sh*t on, I might never speak again'.

There were plenty of ways to market Lisa as a reminder of Elvis.

'People get all kinds of crazy ideas to turn me into a goofball. A whole record of Elvis covers & duets. We can put you in a white suit! Sorry, Britney already took the cake on that one'.

Had Presley ever thought of putting the L.P. out under a band name, like Jakob Dylan did with the Wallflowers?

'I thought about that, or taking Presley off, just using Lisa Marie, but the record company wasn't very happy with the idea. They had other plans. I'm not trying to run away, and I'm not trying to capitalize. I'm just trying to make a f*ckin' record'.

Priscilla said, "The name Presley can be a hindrance & a help". In what ways had it been both to Lisa?

'It's only a hindrance in that I didn't ask for all the attention, so I have a phobia against it. I don't ask tabloids to chase me around every week, but at the same time, I'd never take back any part of who I am or where I came from. I'd never want to be part of anything else. I'm honoured and proud of my family & my dad'.

Had her name helped Presley get a record deal?

'Yeah, it helped me get a foot in the door, but you have to hold your own and again, it's a hindrance, because a lot of attention & pressure is on me. It's a little scary, because folk are either going to love it or they're going to f*ckin' hate my guts. Like, "You're the most despicable, sorry-ass excuse for a Presley that I've ever seen". I'm too extreme, I think, for people to have a mediocre reaction'.

An especially unkind line from one review: 'Her voice belongs in karaoke'.

'You want me to react to that or something? I know it's going to happen. Of course, I obsess on the bad reviews. Nobody wants to hear that sort of crap. Who is this f*ckin' critic? He can bite me. I want to hear him sing. You can print that'.

Most folk wanted to know about Lisa Marie.

'It's the same thing: '3 marriages! Three marriages!"

Presley's ex-husband was involved with the record?

'When you say "ex-husband" you have to be specific. I almost said, "Which ex-husband?" Yeah, Danny and I wrote a couple of songs together. He's the first person that I ever sang in front of & he was the only person who I wrote with for c. 8 yrs, so I wanted him to be on the record'.

Lights Out was about Elvis. Was Lisa reluctant to write about him?

'Very. The last thing I want is to look as if I'm capitalizing on that. I don't want to be famous or superficially rich or some weird novelty. I addressed everything that affected me, and this is obviously important. Everthing that I've written about is pretty autobiographical'.

The song also mentioned Graceland & the 'damn back lawn'. Why had Presley used that phrase?

'Because I couldn't say 'motherf*ckin' back lawn'. It didn't work melodically. The back lawn of Graceland is a graveyard, basically. How many folk have a family grave in the backyard? How many people are reminded of their fate, their mortality, every f*ckin' day? All the graves are lined up & there's a spot there, waiting for me, right next to my grandma'.

Did Lisa Marie plan on being buried there?

'I don't plan on anything. I'm sure I'll end up there or I'll shrink my head and put it in a glass box in the living room. I'll get more tourists to Graceland that way'.

The song was bitter-sweet. Was that how she felt about being a Presley?

'To some degree, it is, but I don't feel bitter--'I'm a Presley & I'm bitter'. There's good and bad with everything'.

Lisa's dad died aged 42, his mum died at 46. Did she think more about death at the age of 35?

'No. When I was writing this album, I went through a period when I wasn't doing very well physically. It was mercury poisoning, from fillings. Everyone has a threshold, but after my divorce from Michael, I was under a lot of stress. My allergies caused craziness--I had my gallbladder removed, I went through hell. I constantly had these weird symptoms that no one could explain. That was probably the worst period in my life, those 2 or 3 yrs'.

Presley's lyrics were hardest on herself -- 'beligerent, needy, a princess'.

'I'm an ar*ehole. Yes, in certain circumstances, I can be any one of those things'.

Lisa Marie also called herself 'a son of a bitch'.

'It's a term that I heard a lot when I was growing up. "C'mere, you little son of a bitch". My family members say that to one another. My Aunt Delia used to live in Graceland. She was a scary woman, very funny. Folk were afraid to be around her. She was an alcoholic diabetic, so she wasn't always in the best mood. Her room was away from the tours but she'd come out to walk her dog then flip off the tourists. They'd come up to her saying, "Are you Aunt Delia?" She'd say, "Hell no! Delia died last night"'.

There was another song, Nobody Noticed It, which seemed like it might've been about Elvis.

'I wrote that to relieve myself of something I saw on TV about him, on the E! True Hollywood Story, which did me in emotionally for days. What made me angry were the interviews with the motherf*ckers who hung around him. These idiots were so disgusting--they helped him go down & were actually worse than he was. It infuriated me. They were trying to take away his dignity, the one thing that was most important to him. I needed to strike back at that. I happened to be going to the studio, when I got the melody in my head then started to cry'.

Did Presley believe in revenge?

'I'm like a lion--I roar. If someone betrays me, I won't be a victim. I don't sulk, I get angry. I immediately go into retaliation but it always comes from insecurity or pain'.

In Priscilla's book, Elvis and Me, she wrote, 'He wasn't the kind of person who'd come out with, 'I'm scared'. He held in his fears & emotions, until at times he'd explode, tearing into anyone who happened to be around'.

'I'm much more like him on that front. That roar--I know it's in the DNA. My mum's very strong, reasonable and caring--I have some of those qualities but the rest is from him. I hear it nonstop from my family: "You're just like him. My god, you're just like your daddy right now". I hear that all the time when I'm in Memphis'.

Had Lisa got a sense of humour about Elvis jokes or comments about her dad shooting out the TV, or was that still too personal?

'No, it's not too personal. Shooting out the television is funny & that makes me laugh. As long as you're not degrading him'.

Did Presley have a favourite Elvis song?

'It's funny, I like the '70s material, because I was around for those recordings. There was some great stuff that never made it to the radio: a song called Mary in the Morning, which I loved. In the Ghetto. I like the darker songs, the sad ones. There's a song called Seperate Ways that was treacherously painful, and How Great Thou Art, when he'd sing that live, there was nothing like it. I'd go to his shows, he was awesome'.

Lisa Marie was 5 yrs old when her parents divorced. How had it changed her life?

'When they divorced, I'd go out on the road more, miss more school, which I liked. Folk say that I didn't get to see him very much, but I was with him quite a bit. All of a sudden a car would show up at school, he was calling for me to go out on the road'.

What was it like, hanging out with Elvis?

'Nocturnal: Go to bed at 4 or 5am then get up at 2 or 3 the next afternoon. It was always a lot of fun. There isn't one bad memory. There was always a lot of energy & life in the house. He was very mischievous'.

Lisa would sit outside his room for hours, waiting for him to get up.

'The only 2 rooms upstairs in Graceland are mine and his. When he slept, he was a bear in hibernation'.

Did Lisa Marie know that Elvis was addicted to pills?

'I was aware of his demis. His temper was getting worse, he was gaining weight, he wasn't happy. I saw him taking different pills, like a potpourri of capsules, but I didn't know what they were. He was obviously not in good shape but he didn't want me to see that, so he'd try to mask it for me'.

Lisa was visiting him at Graceland during '77, when he passed away.

'I was there when he died. I was there for most of the summer. I'm not going to go into his death, the day of the whole thing. Just so you know. I avoid that in all interviews. It's not something I like to capitalize on--particulary for folk's amusement'.

How did her memories compare with the legends about him?

'How much longer are we going to stay on this one? It's not that I don't like talking about him & yes, I could set the record straight. It's just that I'm uncomfortable with divulging anything about him, because people have done that for so long to capitalize on it. I hate those folk so much. It's against my moral code to get attention by discussing him'.

Moving on to Lisa Marie's ex-husbands...

'No--we're going to stay on my dad then'.

Priscilla also wrote that because Elvis spoiled her so much, 'Lisa had trouble learning what was right and wrong'.

'I don't feel like I was spoiled. Anything my father did for me or gave me was done out of love, I took it as that. I'm sure I had moments when I was a snot but my mum was there to smack me back to the other side. Whatever he did, she cleaned up'.

After Presley's parents split up, Priscilla had a boyfriend named Michael Edwards.

'Oh my God, can I use the bathroom before I talk about that sorry-ass?'

He stated that while he was in a relationship with Priscilla, he had sexual feelings for Lisa.

'He's a sick f*ck. I know he wrote a book in which he said that he lusted after my developing body as I got out of a pool. [In his book, Priscilla, Elvis and Me, Edwards wrote, 'I'd had to put an end to our swimming together after one disturbing afternoon in the pool. Lisa had innocently thrown her arms around me & we were jumping up and down. I became aroused. A sick feeling crept slowly into the pit of my stomach. I was craving Lisa sexually'.] He made his attempts at coming into my room & being inappropriate while drunk'.

Presley was a tough kid.

'I'd always had a strength that intimidates people. It's a protection mechanism. In every school, the kids would automatically hate me and think that I was stuck up but I wasn't. I'd make friends with the outcasts. You name it, I'd get in trouble for it. I was in this destructo mode: Anything my mum didn't want me to do - smoking, drinking, drugs, boys, whatever I could get my hands on. I went through a drug phase for 3 yrs'.

Did Lisa Marie have a hard time finding drugs?

'No. Does anyone if they really want them?'

Was Presley sexually active?

'I didn't have sex until I was 15, a fortnight after my 15th birthday, but I was intrigued by sex at a very early age. I think I was a pervert when I was 3. I liked looking up skirts. Body parts intrigued me'.

Did Priscilla keep a close eye on Lisa?

'She watched me closely. After I read her book, I realized why. She'd done things that weren't what your average 14-yr-old would do & I was doing the exact same things'.

How had Lisa Marie and Priscilla become Scientologists?

'I dabbled in it for a bit then ran off to be a spiteful teenager. I rediscovered it when I was 17. I'd spent 3 nights awake, having been on cocaine for 72 hrs. Eventually, my mum kicked me out of the house & made me stay at the Scientology Center. I was drinking, so she handed me over to them in the middle of the night. She wanted them to watch over me and I was happy--I was out of the house & had my own apartment. I had all this freedom. The smartest thing that they ever did was put me to work with drug addicts. That made me productive and responsible. The last time I did a drug for recreation, I was 17. You know what life's going to bring you if you head down that route'.

What did Scientology offer Presley?

'A better understanding of myself & others, sanity and insanity. Good answers--not answers that are enforced but don't really make sense. It's attacked because it's not understood, which annoys me. I mean, I had it all f*ckin' happen to me, but I'm fine. I'm not medicated. I might f*ck up my marriages, but other than that, I'm fine'.

What about the Scientologists belief that humans are descendants of space aliens?

'I never read anything in Scientology about aliens, but I've heard about it. An ex-boyfriend used to go, "Aliens! Aliens!"'.

When Lisa was 17 she met Danny Keough in the church then later married him. What changed when she had a baby?

'I was a tyrant as a kid, but then I had babies and settled down. Recently, in the past 6 yrs, I've got back in touch with my inner tyrant teenager. My friends were all out being crazy at 20, while I had babies. Now they're married & I'm like, "Look at you, you've got it together and I don't!"'.

What's Danny done as a musician?

'He's been in & out of groups. He's had opportunities, but he's his own worst enemy. He likes to sulk and be a tortured soul. He'd rather be anonymous with nobody knowing that he was married to me. He needs confidence'.

Did his lack of confidence stem from having been married to Lisa Marie?

'Very likely. He was overshadowed, buried alive by my mere existence & he resented it'.

In the song Sinking In, Presley said that she didn't treat him well.

'We didn't treat each other well. He can get pretty dark at times. We have that in common'.

Who was darkest?

'We fluctuate. Thank God we don't go off the deep end at the same time, because our kids would be wrecks. He's one of my closest friends. We go on vacations, spend holidays together, take the kids to school every morning'.

Did they give each other romantic advice?

'No. He just shakes his head then laughs at me. I'm his entertainment. "How much of a sh*tstorm can you cause?" He intervened with Michael but even then he wasn't vocal. He just let me know that he wasn't happy about that one'.

Lisa left Danny, an insecure, struggling musician, to marry Michael Jackson, the King of Pop.

'I walked away from Danny and went to Michael, which was stupid. I thought that it'd help, because Michael & I had so much in common, our upbringings. Then it hit me in the face a year later'.

Other than Danny, who knew that Lisa Marie was going to marry Jackson?

'No one except the folk who arranged the wedding'.

Why didn't Presley tell her mum?

'Because I knew that she was against it. She was already saying, "Don't you think this is just good timing for him? Wake up!" but I wouldn't hear anything about it'.

What did Priscilla say when Lisa told her that she'd married Michael?

'She called me casually one day saying, "Ugh, there are helicopters flying over my house, driving me crazy. They're saying that you married Michael Jackson". I was silent then she went, "No, you didn't. Lisa! Tell me". I went, "Yup, I did". I have to say that I got a bit of a kick out of it, just for old times' sake. One more middle finger going up'.

Lots of people suspected that it was a publicity stunt, because he'd been accused of child molestation.

'We met casually at a friend's house, when he immediately disabused me of any preconceived ideas that I had of him. He said, "I know you think this about me, you think that" and I immediately said, "Oh my God, you're so misunderstood!" I forgot who he was within 20 mins, because we were so locked into a conversation'.

Michael Jackson was seductive?

'He's not sexually seductive, but there's something riveting about him. He doesn't let folk see who he is. When he does, it's hard to shake. I got caught up & thought that I was in love with the man. I don't know what else to say'.

When Lisa Marie announced the marriage, she stated in a press release, 'I understand and support him'. Could she explain Jackson?

'Here's the thing: For a while Michael was like the Wizard of Oz, the man behind the curtain. At one time he was really good at manipulating a Howard Hughes type of image: 'He's mysterious, fascinating'. He became this freak & now he can't get out from under it. When you're the king of your own palace, there are no morals or ethics or integrity. Everyone will kiss your ass then give you the push that knocks you over'.

Did Presley and Jackson ever have children join them in bed?

'Never. Never, never, never, never. I never saw him sleep in bed with a child, ever'.

Did Lisa ever see him with photos of nude children?

'Never. Never'.

Did Lisa Marie have any reason to think that he was a child molester?

'If I'd had any reason to suspect that, I would've had nothing to do with the guy. I had no reason to, other than the allegations themselves. The only 2 people who know are Michael & that kid in the room. I've never seen him behave inappropriately. He was great with my kids. He does have a connection with kids, babies. He's a kid, and other kids sense that in him'.

Perhaps it'd help his case if he'd stop saying, "Yes, I sleep with children"?

'I know! Someone should call him & go, "Would you just stop saying that? It's not working for you!"'.

Did Presley discuss having kids with Jackson?

'Yeah. I got out of that one. "I just don't think it's a good idea right now", but I knew that's what he wanted and I knew Debbie Rowe was offering to do it for him while we were married, according to him. She was a nurse who had a crush on him & offered to have his babies'.

Was Michael trying to leverage Lisa into agreeing?

'Kind of. "Debbie Rowe says she'll do it". "Ok, have Debbie Rowe do it!" and it's funny, when I imagined having a child with him, all I could ever see was a custody battle nightmare".

He just wanted to find someone to have his kids?

'I think so, but I don't know'.

Had Lisa Marie watched Jackson's TV interviews with Martin Bashir the previous winter?

'I watched, because I was on the radio tour that week & I was being asked about it everyday. I was like, 'Could there be any worse timing?' I walked away in 1996. It's not something consuming my thoughts anymore'.

When Diane Sawyer interviewed her and Michael, she asked if they'd had sex & Presley was indignant. Could she see why their marriage looked suspicous to folk?

'I can see that, only because that's his thing, not mine. That always upset me. I was married for several years to a bass player nobody knew and before that never dated a celebrity. I never did anything to try to get publicity. I got caught up in Michael's thing, which was manipulation. I was like, "f*ck you people, that's not who I am. Why am I being blamed for a publicity stunt? Oh, I'm Miss Aspiring Singer & now I want a record deal? That's why I'm with him?"'.

It sounded like Lisa thought that Jackson used her.

'I'm not going to say that he did or he didn't. There are things that don't look good, that's all I can say, and most folk saw it at the time except me'.

When had the relationship gone sour for Lisa Marie?

'Not long after Diane Sawyer. I started to wake up & ask a lot of questions. I don't want to go into detail, but it went downhill pretty quickly'.

What about their kiss at the Video Music Awards of 1994? It looked staged and awkward.

'It looked awkward because I wanted out of my skin. At the 11th hr, he says, "I'm gonna kiss you". I was like, "No, I don't want to do that. Do we have to? That's bullsh*t". On the way there I kept saying, "Do we have to?" I squeezed his hand so hard that I cut off the circulation. He wouldn't tell me when it was going to happen'.

Apparently Presley asked Michael for a divorce while he was in hospital recovering from 'exhaustion'.

'Not true. There was a bit of a showdown in the hospital & I didn't understand what was wrong with him. I didn't know what he was up to. When I started asking too many questions about what was wrong, he asked me to leave. This is the real story. He said, "You're causing trouble". The doctors wanted me to go. I freaked out, because it was all too familiar. When he got out, I called him to say, "I want out"'.

Later, when Lisa met Nick Cage, was she thinking of marriage?

'After Michael, I wasn't in a hurry to get married again. Nic was also ending a marriage to Patricia Arquette that wasn't in good shape, but we clicked instantly. He is grand--that's a good word for him. We had somewhat similar realities, both part of famous families, and I admired the f*ck out of him, because he detached himself from his family name [Coppola] & made a career by himself. He and I detected some sort of rebellious spirit in each other. His father, as a wedding gift, gave us a 100-or-200-yr old bottle from the bottom of the ocean & a really nice toast. The whole thing was about how we were both pirate spirits. It was really moving'.

He portrayed Elvis in Honeymoon In Vegas and Wild at Heart.

'There are 45 other films that he did, thank you very much, that don't have anything to do with my dad'.

Did Lisa Marie think that he wanted her because she was Elvis' daughter?

'Here's the answer: I've never seen one Elvis artifact or one piece of Elvis memorabilia that he owns. There was a rumour for a long time that he had an Elvis recording as the f*ckin' outgoing message on his f*ckin' phone machine. I never saw any of that. Sure, he was an Elvis fan. I haven't met many people who've said, "I hate your f*ckin' dad. He was terrible"'.

What went wrong?

'One pirate shouldn't marry another. We'd already broken up then got back together twice. We were together for 2 yrs before we got married & thought that marriage would make us more secure'.

Presley went with him to the premiere of Adaptation just a few days before their divorce.

'We had a fight a few days later, when he had a temper tantrum. He walked out the door, filed for divorce then felt bad. It was just a rampage, basically. He called a couple of days later to say, "Whoops!" He said, "I was in a rage, I'm sorry. I made a mistake. I wish I hadn't done that". I was like, "Dude, we can't do the break-up-get-back-together thing. We're married". He's not surrounded by folk who'd talk him down when he's in a state like that. I hated him afterwards. It was a long time before I'd speak to him'.

A tabloid reported that Lisa threw a $65,000 ring that he gave her into the sea.

'I didn't throw it. Otherwise, that's a true story. We were in a fight, and I said it was over. He took the ring then threw it into the water. We hired a diver but it was 150 ft down & he just shook his head. It was a 6-carat yellow diamond, which Nic replaced 2 days later with a 10-carat yellow diamond'.

Was it strange that they were both giving interviews about their marriage?

'I'm laughing because Nic did an interview with Barbara Walters when he said something to her about my blue eyes. I said to him, "They're f*ckin' green!"'.

Cage gave a TV interview then called her to report what he'd said?

'Yeah. I still care about him a lot. I don't want to have a media war. I'll say, "This is what I said on Diane Sawyer, in case you want to retaliate, but just know that I'll come back. If you say something I don't like, I will f*ckin' nail your ass to the wall!" When Michael and I split up, he said, "Don't talk about me". He never wanted anybody talking about him. I didn't say a word about him but the next 3 interviews that I saw, he was talking about me, so I was like, "All bets are off, dude. You did it"'.

What were Lisa Marie's vices?

'Having friends around. Cigarettes & red wine--but it has to be good red wine. It has to be more than $300 / bottle, because then I don't get as bad a hangover'.

What was Presley like when drunk?

'I'm friendlier, nicer, more tolerant and more patient. Physically, I feel better. I'm not usually patient & tolerant when I'm not drinking'.

Favourite cursing word?

'F*ckin', c*nt and motherf*cker. Curse words are good. When I was drunk & newly out with Nic at a bar, I called him a c*nt at least 6 times but it was kind of a flirtatious thing. If I was seriously calling him that, he would've kicked my ass. My friend Johnny Ramone was with us, who said, "Sailor mouth! If your father could hear you talk like this, what would he think of you?" I don't think it's publicly known, but my father was pretty big on cursing. He wouldn't allow me to curse, but he did'.

Did Lisa read her financial statements?

'Not willingly--I'm forced to. I get angry at how much I'm paying people. It makes me insane. Everytime I see a f*ckin' financial statement, I want to fire folk. There was this crazy woman that I brought into my circle, who pulled a Machiavellian maneuver and tried to take my empire down by backstabbing people & spinning a whole web--just unbelievably evil'.

What were Lisa Marie's sexual tastes?

'Probably 'porn style'. I'm a little dark on the subject. I like it rough, the way they do things in porn movies'.

Had Presley ever wished that she was a lesbian?

'Sure. I think I'd be much better off as a lesbian. My best friend is also my assistant, and she's been with me for 8 yrs. I feel like, 'Damn! If I were gay & I could've been with you, we would've been perfect''.

What would Lisa do differently if she got married again?

'I'm going to become a eunuch or a monk--nonsexual and nonfunctioning. I'm going to--you know what? I can't say what the hell I'm going to do, to be honest'.

If Lisa Marie's kids were going to write a tell all about her, what was the worst they could say?

'Just that mum went through me like water. If I get wed again, I'll stay married. I don't know if I really thought I'd stay married with the last couple. I'm whimsical about things. I get caught up in the moment. It's the one area where I'm naive'.

Were her kids having a tough time because they were Presleys?

'My daughter is 14 & some kids are starting to give her cr*p. "What are you complaining about? You rich litte--". I want to choke that kid, by the way. If there's a little kid in school that's being an ar*ehole, I want to kick the kid's ass. If I could, I'd go scare them. It's at the point where my kids won't tell me what's happening'.

Did Lisa want more kids?

'I'd like a couple more'.

If she didn't have someone to be the father--

'Are you kidding me? No, I will not go to a sperm donor. I could ask Debbie Rowe to be a surrogate for me'.

Lisa Marie was still fond of Danny and Nic. Maybe she'd get back together with one of her exes.

'With me, you never f*ckin' know, do you? God! You know what? I'm not going to say never about anything again'.

Lisa Marie Presley might've been a chip off the old block but even the King would've been all shook up to find out about his only daughter's secret new job -- bagging fish 'n' chips out of the back of a van in the quiet wee English village where she lived. The daughter of Elvis Presley took to the grease like a local when she volunteered to work the 'Mr. Chippy' van of her friends Kim & Justin Scales, who also owned local pub the King's Arms, in the southeast England village of Rotherfield where Lisa and her husband regularly lifted a Guinness & played darts with the local gentry.

It was a long way from Graceland, the Memphis mansion where she and Priscilla had just made a surprise visit to a candlelight vigil marking the 35th anniversary of Elvis' death. Lisa Marie flew in from England, where she, guitarist husband Michael Lockwood & 3 of their 4 children had lived for the previous couple of years. Fleeing the paparazzi in Los Angeles, they bought a $13 million mansion on 90 acres in Rotherfield during 2010, where they lived with 3 of their kids in the estate house not far from the former home of L. Ron Hubbard, the founder of Scientology. Despite its proximity, Presley had apparently quit the controversial church that she'd once credited with helping her kick drug addiction.

Working at a 'chippy', -- The Sun labeled her the 'The Queen of Rock 'n' Sole' -- was the latest evidence that English country life suited the singer, who'd enthusiastically joined in community activities, including taking part in a fun run to raise money for a local children's hospice. Lisa also donated a photo of her dad that fetched over $11,000 at an auction to raise money for a charity that granted wishes for children with life-threatening diseases.

"I lived in the same neighbourhood for 17 yrs but I didn't even know a neighbour", Lisa Marie told BBC Radio 2 that week, stating that her English ones were far nicer than "self-absorbed" Californians. "When I moved here I was getting notes and flowers. That's what I love about it. It's simple, it's not flash, it was a quality of life that I needed, said Presley, 44.

Not that she'd be slinging fish 'n' chips full-time, as Kim Scales told the Daily Mail: "No way! She got the fish all upside down & was totally cack-handed". Kim, who ran the pub where Lisa liked to hang out, said that she didn't come in "all glammed up", mingling with the locals at the bar. "She likes to see how we live and experience it. We were laughing, because the customers didn't know it was her. She really enjoyed it".

Lisa Marie Presley, whose 3rd L.P. Storm & Grace, produced by 12-time Grammy winner T-Bone Burnett, had come out the previous year, said "I'll start the tour at the end of August and it'll kind of go on until Thanksgiving". Did she enjoy being on tour?

"I love it, favourite thing - ever. I just love the interaction with the fans & I like to see what they have to say. I love my relationship with my fans. It's just a nice sort of exchange of energy between me and them. Then after, I love meeting them, talking to them...".

Were there any negatives, like the busy schedule, the pressure...

"It can get tiring, but physically I'm not really a big complainer, so I more love it than anything bad about it".

The 1st single from Lisa Marie's latest album You Ain't Seen Nothin' Yet, seemed like a very personal song.

"I've never written a non personal song. I mean - it's there, autobiographical, something from my heart, so yes. It's no different than any other song that I've written. It was how I was feeling at that moment. I don't like to go into specifics about what my songs are about. It's just something I went through then wrote about it. It's kind of explanatory, but I also like people to make what they want from it".

When Lisa wrote a song, where did it come from? What was its source?

"My life, what I've seen, what I've felt. Something that inspired me, something that upset me or something I went through, it's just kind of an outlet, it's very therapeutic for me. I've always liked writing, since I was a child, poetry or anything... I just use it as an outlet for myself".

In which song did Presley find herself the most?

"In all my songs really. I mean - when I write a sheet or whatever that's on my mind, what's happening with me. I find how to describe something in a way that could be universal for anybody to relate to. It's very seminal. They all are me - autobiographical, something that's going on, that I've seen, or felt, or something that someone else is going through".

How did Lisa Marie handle her celebrity life in the public eye, as the daughter of Elvis Presley?

"I'm one of those people who're a little bit old fashioned. When I grew up it wasn't so popular that most folk avoided trying to be in the tabloids, trying to be in the papers all the time & being constantly discussed, so I'm kind of a bit old fashioned. I try to just keep it very separated. When I'm not working, and when I'm not out there I'm very much a mother & a wife, and we have a life that is very separate & normal.

Then when I'm working you switch gears and go into that. I keep it very separated. My mum raised me that way & my father was the same. He'd retreat afterwards - he'd have spells in the public eye, doing his touring when he needed to, but then he'd go back to Memphis, which was kind of his safe place, where he'd sort of retreat to. That's kind of how I do it - live normally when I'm not working".

Did Lisa think that it was harder for her to prove herself as an artist, because of who she was - of who her dad was?

"Yes, I will say that. That's accurate, because there's a constant compromising. I mean it definitely would be easier, I think, in any other position, if I didn't have such a love for music I'd be something else. There's a constant pressure that wouldn't be on anyone else, obviously. I just look through the folk and they're out there, that just love my music. I helped them, changing their lives in some ways & that keeps me going.

I hear the stories; I hear what they want to tell me, if some song changed their life. Those things really matter to me. If I'm helping people then that makes me happy. It's not definitely going to be easy for me, because it's always that "she's not him". Those things happen, I know it's always there, but also there are those people out there for whom that didn't matter, that just love my music, and that's what keeps me going".

Presley's dad was the King of Rock 'n' Roll & she was married to the King of Pop. Did she see herself as a part of music royalty?

"I'm not the kind of person that'd call myself that. Yeah, I'd never see myself that way".

Lisa Marie was aware of it though?

"Yes, I understand but I'm not someone who'd go around proclaiming it for myself, I'd say that. I understand it, and that's fine".

Lisa was often surrounded by paparazzi. Was there a place where she could hide to fully relax?

"Oh, yes. I'm pretty good at keeping it quiet. I don't do those things like calling them, telling them where I'm going & that's kind of what folk do now. Things changed, I'm not quite sure when, but it kind of turned into people starting to call them, that was a trend that started, and hasn't stopped. I think they love those folk, but I don't do that. If they see me they get me, if they don't... I kind of stay out of the way. I don't go where they hang outs a lot. Sometimes I do, but there's plenty of places to go where they're not able to see me all the time. I'm old fashioned about that as well".

Did Presley plan to write a book about her life one day?

"I wouldn't say no. I don't have any plans at the moment, but my favourite thing in the world is to read other people's autobiographies, I love it. I thought about it & I'm still going through the things, so when I come to another end, maybe one day. It's not out of the question. I would like to have my life out there in my own words, rather than speculations".

Lisa Marie Presley had released her L.P. 'Now What?' Was it the name of one of the songs, or was it a statement?

'It's the name of a song'.

Dealing with now what?

'No, I think it's representative of me in that it's seemingly sarcastic and sort of bold & had an attitude, but yet if you hear the song, it's very vulnerable and soul searching to some degree'.

When had Lisa Marie decided that she was a singer?

'I think that was when I sang a song in front of a vocal teacher one day -- I was doing scales. I wasn't really serious. I just wanted to do it really bad & I'd do piano scales all the time'.

How old was Lisa?

'In my teens, probably 19. I said 'OK, I'm going to sing one day' then I said, 'I'm going to sing and I don't want you to watch me. I'm going to turn around with my back to you & I'm going to sing, just tell me what you think later. So I sang a verse in a chorus out of a song and had she - who I very much respected at the time - not had such a reaction to me doing that, I would've probably crumbled & died and gone away somewhere, but she happened to jump up & say 'Oh my God'. Then she got her husband and I went in with my ex-husband, we did a demo of an Aretha Franklin song. That's kind of when I realized, I gave myself a high challenge'.

Did Priscilla like the idea?

'I don't think at first, no. She was scared, worried, as a mother should be, understandably worried about me'.

She knew that once she'd come forward as Lisa Marie Presley, with that name she'd be judged by a different standard, so she rolled some dice.

'I think I was more naive on that front than one would expect. I've been a huge music lover, it's always had a huge impact on me. I want to write, I want to sing. I want to do the same thing for others, hopefully have my music do that for others one day, not realizing what I sort of had to climb. I had an idea a little bit, but I think that I underestimated the whole thing'.

Was Presley surprised by the reaction to her 1st CD?

'I was. I was surprised. I was surprised a lot'.

Favourably or unfavourably?

'Favourably surprised. More surprised at the reaction to the 1st CD -- they were surprised that I made a good record, which was surprising to me'.

That they were surprised.

'Yeah. I'm thinking, I know music. I think they thought maybe pop. It was surprising to see what preconceived idea they had of me in order to come to the conclusion that I'm a bad record or a poppy or a sellout record'.

How well did it do?

'I don't know the current status. It went gold & I was very proud of that. I don't think that I'm a top 40 artist in any way. I don't think I'm that mainstream, so it's a little bit of a challenge to find me, because there's only certain types of music right now'.

Hard to go gold if you're not a top 40 artist.

'Yeah. I don't know how that works. It seems like it happens really fast when you're going for a top 40. It's a very quick climb. It used to be long, long ago that you could make records and sort of build your way & evolve as an artist'.

Now you're a golden oldie the day that it comes out.

'If it doesn't do a certain amount, yes'.

It's extraordinary. Every time I see Lisa Marie, she looks more like her dad.

'I see it sometimes when I'm performing, to be honest with you, but it's not intentional at all. I think we all have traits of our parents regardless and that's when I see it'.

One of the songs was called Dirty Laundry, a Don Henley tune, dealing with the TV news, business & sensational coverage. Was that a bit autobiographical?

'For me, I think it's more just pointing out the general state of affairs in terms of what our entertainment is now. It wasn't a direct attack on the media -- an attack on the media per se. It was more just me trying to point out what our entertainment is. There's a fine line now where there's legitimate media and news -- it just seems over the top, whether it be reality shows, or cameras & an ambulance when someone's -- these shows make me physically ill watching on TV. It just kind of points out the general state of affairs, I think, the lyrics in the song and therefore that's why I picked it'.

Lisa thought that it was a sad state of affairs.

'I do'.

The mainstream media, the tabloids, they'd been rough on Presley.

'They've been rough. They're really rough. I have to say that I don't know if they liked it that the record was successful, because they went on a campaign. As soon as I got on my 1st tour -- they were quiet through all that last media then when I got on my first tour, they started doing this whole slander campaign -- they came out trying to make me look like my father in the end. It seemed like there was a campaign aiming towards making me look like I'm miserable & hugely overweight, doctoring photos and doing this whole number. It was like somebody deliberately sat there & went 'How can we sabotage this and make her look like that?' That one blew me away'.

It sold papers.

'Yes. It blows me away that they can make me the size of a car on the cover & get away with it'.

Did Lisa Marie ever used to being hounded by the paparazzi? Did that ever get old hat?

'I do get used with that?'

It goes with the territory?

'I think it's more in Los Angeles that it happens. It goes with the territory more here. You tend to get a lot used to it I suppose'.

Lisa didn't get it as much in other places?

'No, they're really here. If you go to a hospital here -- a friend of mine was dying and they have their black cars with black windows, sitting in the hospital parking lot at Cedars -- when you go to valet'.

How do they know you're going to be there?

'They're waiting for any celebrity or tragedy to happen'.

They wait at the hospital...

'They sit in the valet. I have this weird radar for them. I can hear & see them when I walk out. I went to visit a friend and more than once have gone to Cedars for various reasons -- nothing serious -- & I continuously see that, yes'.

What did Presley make of the coverage of her ex-husband?

'It's so delicate and it's such a hot stove that it's one of those things I'd love to chat with you about but anything you say at this point is going to add'.

Did it annoy Lisa Marie to see the focus on someone that she cared about, probably still cared about?

'To be honest with you it's kind of a blessing that this is happening in that I don't have to say anything right now, because there's a trial going on'.

I mean, emotionally though.

'Emotionally it's never easy to watch anybody go through something really difficult'.

Because Lisa had been a staunch defender of him.

'Well, I'm not going to talk about it'.

I mean as a person & a husband -- we aren't dealing with the charges or anything.

'At one point I was'.

A supporter, but now Presley was neutral?

'I'm just benign really'.

Was Lisa Marie going to tour again?

'I am. I sort of did it all backwards last time. I did all the press thing, threw everything in then I kind of got used -- you're supposed to do it the other way round, see that you speak to the audience and see what your music does to people, but I kind of did the reverse'.

What had Lisa been doing since that CD? Where had she been?

"Where have I been? I've been writing. Writing this one, pretty much".

Presley wrote all the songs except for the Henley song?

"Right. I co-wrote one of the songs on this -- but most of it's all me. The rest of it".

Did Lisa Marie like writing on her own?

"I do. My contribution is the writing, the lyrics & the melodies.

It takes that long?

"It took c. 8 months then you go through the mixing and that 'I don't like this and you need to change that' process".

Lisa sold 85% of the Presley estate, which led to a lot of controversy.

'OK. Well, it's kind of a misconception in the way it was -- it's a very complicated business deal. It took me weeks to understand it, but it was misleading the way the press ran it, because it is complex. There's 2 separate entities; Elvis Presley Enterprises & Elvis Presley Estate. Now, 85% -- what we did is we merged with Sillerman. He bought 85% of the Enterprises, which is different from the Estate. That's mine, his thing's mine, everything's still mine and in order. He has the 85%, but I also still have 15%.

It was a united decision, because pretty much things don't stay the same. They either go up or down & we've known for a very long time that we need to merge and get with someone, to take it to a bigger, better place than we were able to do on our own, standing alone. It was a united decision that's been deliberated over for years. What happened is that the money that came back got reversed, a lot of it going right back into stock, to form a bigger new company, merging with Sillerman, who's got a very good track record, he knows what he's doing".

Elvis Presley Enterprises includes what?

"Name, likeness, image, music, films, merchandise, things like that".

Lisa Marie still owned 15% of that.

"I own 15% of that, but he & I are partners, and my mother is on the board. There's a new company now, which is going public & my mum's on the board of directors for that. Everyone who works at the Estate and who has worked at the Estate this entire time is still in order, intact, everyone's still got their jobs. We all made the decision, because we wanted to grow bigger & better".

No one lost anything.

"No one lost anything. The CEO is still there, everyone is still there. My family is taken care of. It was a move that we had to make to grow and oddly enough the money that came out of the sale thing, went right back into the preferred stock in a bigger company, which means that we believe he can take it to a bigger, better place".

The home & those kinds of things, just remain with Lisa.

"The home is absolutely mine. Everything in it is mine. All of his personal things are mine".

Lisa Marie never had to work then?

"Technically, no".

Presley worked because she wanted to, rather than needing the income?

"Right. I work because I think that I wouldn't feel good about myself unless I was contributing. It's not as selfish -- I'm not a vain or self-centred person in any sense, but I feel like I need to contribute. I am involved in -- prior to singing, in a lot of different things; family housing, educational programs. I've gotten involved in stopping the -- anti-drugging of kids campaigns, but for me, music is just another outlet'.

How did the story of the sale get so screwed up then?

"Because it was very complex, and folk couldn't get past the headlines. 'Sold, 85% sold, it looked like the estate & I sold everything but I'm going 'No, no, no, no'. Business-wise, we're getting a huge thumbs-up, that was an awesome move but personally it just came across wrong, because estate sold sounds like estate. Estate is mine'.

How big is the tourism industry there at the estate?

"It's quite substantial. It's good'.

Graceland draws a lot of people. The interest in Elvis seems to grow.

"True".

His records sell in the UK.

"Yes".

Was there a new audience all the time? Who was finding Elvis?

"That's what we're hoping. I'd imagine that more people are just kind of sick of what's happening right now and they're kind of looking back to what was, I don't know. We just recently went to #1 in England again, which is amazing, but the bottom line is, music speaks & music tells the story".

How did Lisa appreciate his talent?

"God, there's a documentary coming out in May. It's called Presley by the Presleys, and I'm normally not involved in things like that, I've stayed away from it, but this is done so well that -- it's done in only his voice, my mum's, mine, my grandparents, his mother. It's through all of our voices, it's not someone narrating".

Presley by the Presleys.

"Yes. It's quite fascinating & I learned so much about him watching, because there was footage pulled that no one's ever seen. Which is interesting".

For what kind of distribution, for tv?

"It's going to be for television. I think it's a CBS special".

What did Lisa Marie think as she looked at Elvis, heard him? What was the appeal, what did he have?

"What he had was completely uncontrived, what he was, was what he was. Nowadays you have machines and PR, images being created, you have all these things going on, a lot of people working to create different things but with him, there was none of that. There was nothing -- everything you saw & folk appreciated about him, he was that or more off stage. There was nothing contrived or preconceived about anything he was about or did and I think people feel that genuineness, which doesn't happen very often anymore. You've got masses of folk that are behind everyone, making an image, making everything".

He only had the Colonel managing him, and Elvis did the act. What was special about his voice, his singing, his music?

"I can't answer that. I mean, I can tell you that".

As a listener?

"His soul, spirit came through that voice & that moves people -- there's like an aesthetic plane it hits somewhere, where it's a very spiritual thing, and I really feel like he penetrated through his voice".

How was Priscilla doing?

"She's doing very well".

Acting?

"No, she's on this board now, so she's quite busy with that".

They were all like business folk.

"I guess so. She's always been, but now she's also on the board of MGM, so she's behind the scenes doing a lot".

Still pretty?

"Beautiful".

Priscilla: 'After your dad died, it was either sell Graceland or give it up to the state'.

"To go there now, it's like comforting to see it in its original form, never touched, but on the other hand, it's sort of heartbreaking to go there & look at -- it's just a shell now of what it was".

Priscilla: 'It's a house now. It's not the home that it was, but trying to recreate that without Elvis, it really isn't a home'.

Did Priscilla know that her daughter could sing?

Priscilla: 'Lisa, for the longest time, didn't sing. I had no idea that she even had a voice. She'd play music like most teenagers, but I remember even telling her to turn the music down it was so loud. She was probably practicing all of those years'.

When did it happen.

Priscilla: 'She wanted to start singing, I guess maybe c. 10 yrs ago. I tried to encourage her to take lessons, because obviously she has some big shoes to step in and my concern was that she'd try to do this with no training whatsoever. She eventually started taking voice lessons but I don't even know if she needs them'.

Was Priscilla surprised when she heard the finished product?

Priscilla: 'Well, not really. I think she's very talented. I'm probably her biggest fan'.

Lisa Marie wrote a song called Raven inspired by Priscilla.

"It's for her".

What was Raven?

"It's just me -- I wrote a song for her & one Christmas, I asked, 'Will you come out to listen to this song in my car? I didn't write one for her on my 1st record, because I didn't get around to it then I got really inspired and our relationship has evolved so much that I was inspired to write a song about her, for her. I took her outside then played it for her & she started crying and now it's her favourite song on the record, of course.

On the record there's a tape recording of me aged 3 that I start playing in the beginning of the song, which is me, she's making me sing. She said, "Sing it right" or something like that & I start pouting and singing -- it kind of shows -- then the song happens then at the end it comes back with her & I arguing. At the end of that I sort of end it with 'I think I love you', which shows the entirety of the evolution of our relationship".

What did Raven mean?

"I'm just referring to her as that. That's what she inspired me to refer her to as...".

 Interesting bird.

"It's nice -- it's an interesting bird. Yes".

Complicated bird.

"Aye".

Was it a blessing to be a Presley?

"I was trying to figure out a way to answer that question, where it didn't sound like -- the last thing that I ever would be or sound like is a whining celebrity in any sense. I agree that's not a good thing. The thing is, in any kind of situation that you're in, where you're high profile -- you get a lot of attention and to the degree that you get that attention is the same degree or more that you're going to get attacked.

So as much as folk out there are rooting for you & wanting you to do well, there's a half or larger number that want to you to fall. So it's finding that balance and not -- without whining or saying I'm not very grateful of who I am & where I've come from. It's still something that you end up dealing with things that other people don't necessarily have to deal with, and you're under attack more".

Were there days when Lisa was sorry that she was a Presley?

"No. I'm never sorry. It's just that you never can let your guard down on how to handle things. Constantly, things will happen & you have to figure out how to combat it".

Why did Lisa Marie think that folk wanted to see famous people or the offspring of famous people fail?

"I don't -- it's really interesting, because I've recently talked to a couple of other ones, I won't mention their names but historical figures' offspring, they're petrified to take this route. I said 'You can watch me, I'll be the prototype. I'll just -- I'll do it. Whatever I do, you do the opposite. I'm going to go out and do it, because I don't want fear to stop me'. I don't know why -- first there's the comparison thing. You run into that then you run into climbing the -- it's something that's not easy for someone. It's easy in that it opens the door. After that you're on your own".

Could Lisa see any continuum in her own life, as the daughter of the most famous singer in the world, who then married the most famous singer in the world. See a connection?

"Yes. Probably, I'm not into psycho-analysis, but there's probably something in my looking -- I had to experience that & I think that there was some of that in the back of my mind, probably".

No regrets over it?

"No. I don't have any regrets".

The decision Presley made -- a couple of other quick things on Michael. Did she feel sorry for him?

"I can't answer. Don't do this to me. Please".

Lisa Marie didn't want to talk about it.

"I don't want -- I just want to stay out of it".

Lisa could be sorry.

"Well -- like I said, I don't like to see anybody go through anything horrendous like that. I'm sure he's not having a good time".

Folk bugged Presley about it a lot. I'm going to stop bugging but. I don't want to bug you.

"Every time. Usually it's a last question but, yes".

Because it's an emotional thing and I'd try to...

"I understand".

We'd try to put ourselves in your place, how would I deal with it if a famous ex of mine was going through this.

"I totally understand what you're doing, but at the same time, if I say anything, it's going to be blown up and taken -- anything about him right now is such a hot -- it's a hot subject".

No matter what Lisa Marie said it was misconstrued.

"Good or bad, it'll be taken out of context right, because anything about him...".

One other thing, did Lisa follow the story?

"No".

Presley removed herself?

"I'm completely removed from the whole thing".

How did Priscilla handle it when Lisa Marie got all of that attention being married to Michael Jackson?

Priscilla: 'Concern. I think any mother would be concerned. Obviously, if my daughter's happy then I don't have any problem, but she's very strong willed'.

Wonder where she got that from?

Priscilla: 'I don't know'.

Was Lisa happy for a time?

Priscilla: 'I think so'.

What was Lisa Marie's favourite song?

"I think that there's a song called 'Idiot' that I like. It's not a nice song".

Was Presley referring to anyone in writing it?

"I was but I don't like to talk about who I was writing about".

There was someone who'd know who Lisa was writing about.

"I hope so".

Was it a he?

"Yes, it's a he".

When he heard it, he'd know.

"I hope so".

Dedicated to him, the idiot.

"Everyone wants to know who that song is about, which is really funny, but it'd ruin it for other people, because it's a good song".

How was Lisa Marie's daughter doing?

"My daughter is exceptionally incredible".

Presley didn't look old enough to have a 15-yr-old daughter.

"They age you, children. What happens?"

How old was Lisa when she was born?

"21".

She was a model already?

"She's taken it on, yes".

How had that happened?

"A very big struggle on my end, in that she really wanted to start, she really was interested in modeling & I had a very big dilemma about it, because I don't want her to be shallow or fall into something, and I had to make the decision 'Do I stop my child?' Making a child wait until they're 18 or 20 to do what they want to do is kind of stupid, because then it's down time, so they get into trouble along the way & they lose their way anyway".

Stifling them.

"Right. I didn't want to stifle her, but didn't want her to head into a destructive profession. Anyway, thankfully she's got a good head on her shoulders, she's handling it very well, and as much as she works & as much as she's in school, it's my responsibility to keep it balanced".

Did she get a lot of work?

"She gets tons -- she gets a lot of work. She's with Christian Dior right now, flies to Paris to do that".

Wasn't that a little grownup?

"Yes".

Did she do any specialty modeling? Was there something that they liked her in, certain kinds of things?

"She's kind of doing a lot of stuff overseas, which I'm happy about, as opposed to in America".

Why?

"Because I don't really want her, I don't want vultures coming out yet. I'm trying to keep them back as long as possible".

Because she's going to get it, right?

"Yes. I'm preparing her for that. She watches me and she's got a really good head on her shoulders".

Mature?

"Very mature, very smart, sees right through you".

Where did she grow up?

"Mostly in Los Angeles".

Which school? She goes to a regular school, she goes to Europe then comes back?

"Yes. She'll go to Europe for a couple of days, or a week, get a lot of work done over there then stay in school for months".

Did Lisa Marie have someone with her when she was over there?

"Absolutely. Her dad goes with her".

Who was he?

"Her father is Danny Keogh".

Was Presley still friends with him?

"Yes. In fact, he's playing bass in my band".

It was nice that Lisa had a good relationship with an ex.

"It's great. We're like brother & sister".

Was he a great dad?

"He's a great dad".

Who was Michael Lockwood?

"He's my musical director".

Was he the new man in Lisa Marie's life?

"Aye".

He wasn't an idiot?

"No".

How had that come about?

"That was just an evolution of being together working for a long time. I just kind of happen to have had a crush on him from the minute that I met him personally, but yes".

Serious?

"It's serious, yes. I don't want to have anything else".

There was no other person in Presley's life?

"No".

Was Lisa going to get engaged?

"I don't know".

Could Lisa Marie envision it?

"Yes, I could envision spending the rest of my life with him, easily".

What was special about guitarist Michael Lockwood?

"I just had this idea that we'd be perfect together and I don't think I realized how right I was when I thought that. Just everything. We're together 24-7. We do everything together. I've never had a relationship like this before. It took me 36 yrs, mind you".

Would Presley say that it was the great love?

"Yes".

Would Elvis have liked him?

"Aye".

Why?

"Because my mum likes him & I can go off of the fact that I know that -- I haven't met anybody that doesn't like him. He's not somebody that people don't like. He doesn't have that kind of vibe about him".

Did Lisa think that Elvis would've been hard on guys that she dated?

"Whew, yes, yes".

He would've been controlling?

"Um-hum".

Did Lisa Marie often think back to that terrible day, because she was there when he passed away".

"Aye".

Did Presley think back to it a lot?

"I don't usually go into this either. That's something that I haven't talked about. Yes, I was. It's something that I tend to stay away from getting into, because once I open that door, every time that's all that's going to be brought up to me".

Did Lisa worry about becoming addicted to substances, because that's genetic.

"No. I don't. I've never been...".

Never felt susceptible to it?

"No, never".

Because it's genetic. Lisa Marie was smart, she knew that -- like the trait to alcoholism being passed on.

"Right. Yes, that's a theory, um-hum. I've never had an addiction to anything".

Priscilla: 'My daughter? Surprisingly enough, I don't think that she really knew the impact nor did she really know what had happened'.

Nine is a tough age.

Priscilla: '9 is very tough and it was very difficult for her to believe. I remember that she took a golf cart that she would ride around Graceland. She was out with her friend & I thought that was a little odd but then again, remembering the age. I preferred her to be out than in the house, because it was very depressing'.

How big was the tour?

"I'm kind of comfortable in 2, 1, 3,000 a night type of places. I like house of blues a lot, so that's kind of what we have, we stick around".

They kept Presley working a lot. Did she like going out for extended periods?

"Two -- yes, 2 to 3 weeks I'm out. Two nights on, 1 night off, typically".

Did that take Lisa away from her daughter?

"No, they come out with me or I plan a tour around when they're going to be out of town or something, so we're never apart for more than a week".

Was there anything about Lisa Marie's singing that was like her dad's?

"He was technically emotionally brilliant. I'm kind of skidding around'.

Elvis didn't write, though.

"No, no, he didn't. I'm sure he could have. I don't think it was at that time, artists weren't really writing their own music. I don't think anybody was but there are some tones that I can get going that could be similar, here and there'.

Elvis changed music, didn't he?

"Oh, yes he did".

He set a trend in American music.

"What a cross to bare at the time, in the '50s. Breaking through the pressure. I don't even know what kind of music was happening. He had a tidal wave come at him for changing -- doing all the things he did. It's kind of hard for people -- that's where this documentary is good, because it's kind of hard for folk to -- nowadays you can pretty much do anything -- no one's shocking anybody anymore. At that time it was very, very conservative & what he did was completely -- it blew everybody".

They wouldn't show the bottom half of him on the Ed Sullivan show. It was a riot. Did Presley like being involved in the business end?

"In terms of the Estate?"

Lisa was involved in decisions...

"Yes".

... or 15%, Lisa Marie liked that?

"Yes, I do. I've been sort of bred to do that since I was 16. My mum's made me go to meetings since I was 16 to get me used to the whole idea, so yes. It's a big responsibility for me and I take it very seriously".

Presley was the inheritor wasn't she?

"Aye".

Because her parents were divorced.

"Yes".

Priscilla was involved but it was Lisa's inheritance. That was a big responsibility.

"It is".

It was going to pass on to Riley.

"It is. Yes".

Did Lisa Marie feel it?

"Yes. When I make a decision like I made, yes".

That was Presley's decision?

"It was -- no, it was actually all of us. I mean, we all -- believe me. It was a lot of phone calls, a lot of meetings, a lot of back & forth but when my mother opened the house originally, it was the graves first. Everybody screamed at her for doing that then when she opened the house she got screamed at. If you make a move, you're going to upset people, so you have to -- it is a big responsibility".

Do Lisa keep in touch with his many old friends?

"I don't -- I heard you had a show".

Oh, we did, great show.

"Was it good?"

Great show. Boy, they loved Elvis.

"Right. I'm in touch with Jerry Shilling and Joe Esposito. Those are the 2 that I still talk to".

They were army buddies?

"Yes".

They go back -- continue that thing of a legacy with Lisa Marie's dad.

"True".

He was part of their life every day.

"Aye".

How close a father was he to Lisa?

"Very".

Because Elvis traveled a lot.

"When he wasn't traveling, he was with me. I was with him as much as he could be".

Did Elvis want Lisa Marie to sing?

"He wanted me to know how to play piano & I know that when he was away my mum had me sing into a tape recorder then sent it to him. So, maybe. I'd have to ask her".

What's Graceland like? Did Lisa spend much time there?

"I go there 2 to 3 times / yr, and as much as I can. I still have family there, so I sort of like to inject life into the house every now & then. Have us all go up there to eat".

What did a tourist get at Graceland?

"Usually they pay for a ticket and they can -- there's property across the street, there's a plane. There's museums across the street from the house itself. There's the grave site, there's several different things".

There's the plane?

"There's the Lisa Marie across the street".

Elvis is buried there too?

"Yes".

So, you can visit the burial site.

"Aye".

Folk can go through the house?

"Yes. Everything but upstairs is open".

The living quarters.

"Yes".

"Everyone had horses & golf carts. One person would get on then everyone would get on then it'd be like a convoy of golf carts. It was always crazy".

So, we're trying to keep up with him, which is kind of hard to do, because he was, Elvis could be pretty wild.

"I also led the convoy when I got old enough to hit the pedal".

Priscilla: 'Lisa started doing the same thing with her little friends. She had a golf cart and would drive all over Graceland at a very young age, like, 5 or 6-yrs-old'.

"I had c. 5 friends up there & some cousins".

She had her own little entourage of people. We could ride and did, we were probably really lucky that nobody got hurt.

"We'd all sort of congregate when I'd come to town & everyone would get a golf cart".

Did the father of Presley's daughter like Michael Lockwood?

"They're very good friends. I never thought it would happen. It's the most amazing thing. We've been through so much. When I was 19, I knew to have my children with Danny, and no matter what'd happen, in our lives we could always be connected & be OK, regardless. It's been very difficult at times, being with other people and having him be OK with the fact that we're so close & what we still have. I understand that we have a very amazing responsibility together, that we brought this in here together and because of whatever happened with us, it has nothing to do with them. So we still raise our kids together & that's kind of a tall order for someone...".

Lockwood had to understand that Lisa Marie might talk to Danny a lot, be friends with him a lot.

"Right. Michael is the musical director and Danny's playing bass, so I mean, it's kind of one of those things...".

Lockwood was his boss?

"Basically, yeah. They all work together, we all work together, but yeah, there's a great thing going on, & I'm really thankful, because it took a long time for that to happen".

Lisa wrote Raven for her mum. Had she ever written a song for her dad?

"There was a song on my first record called Nobody Noticed It that I wrote for him".

Now What? was about what?

"Now What?" is just a vulnerable me struggling with something that was at one time really important to me that I tried to be a part of, that I wasn't -- didn't feel like I caught it. So I'm kind of talking about that, if that makes any sense".

Did writing come easily to Presley?

"Aye".

It flows?

"Yes".

Did Lisa Marie throw away much?

"No. Not that often".

A lot of writers just wrote, tore things up then went on to other things but Lisa stayed with it?

"Pretty much".

Still a Scientologist?

"Aye, Sir".

What attracted Presley to Scientology? Tom Cruise was one.

"Yes. I think that what attracted me was that I just knew that it was for me, because it wasn't something that was going to make me believe in something -- they just had the answers. They explained life, people, me, that made sense to me, that worked, that answered a lot of my questions".

Did Lisa Marie use it a lot? Did she go to meetings?

"There's no meetings, but I definitely use and refer to, the man was a genius, I don't know what to say other than that".

Larry King interviewed him during the '60s, about a science fiction book that he wrote.

"Was it print or TV?"

On TV in Miami.

"Wow! That's very interesting".

It's historic. They should've saved the tape.

"You should've saved it".

Like kinescope, because the Scientologists look up to him as he's the founder of the faith. Is it called a faith?

"It was a religion. It was bona fide, it was acknowledged as a religion by the IRS".

Why did Lisa think that it was controversial?

"I think that anything that's young and growing quickly is scary & controversial, and anything with religion is also a bit sketchy. When you have that on it, organized & usually there's different things but the bottom line is that what's in there and what he says isn't something that you have to believe. You read it, you check it out, you see if it's not the truth & it works exactly as he said. He figured out a lot and that it makes sense, therefore it answers a lot of questions. It brings a lot of sanity in my life".

Presley wanted to tour. Hopefully there'd be another CD. Did she want to keep on singing?

"I do".

Other goals? Did Lisa Marie want to act?

"No, I don't want to act".

Not like her dad did?

"Like I said, my contribution is through my writing & my music, I'm not someone who just wants attention -- not that he was, but nowadays folk are doing everything".

If Lisa married Michael Lockwood, did she want kids?

"Yes. Very much. That's definitely something that I want".

So did Michael?

"Yes".

Presley was 36.

"Yes, 37".

She'd have to get wed soon. Lisa Marie didn't want to wait until she was 42, 43?

"I don't want to distract -- yes, we just don't want like to get the wrong attention right now, so we just do our thing".

Would it get the wrong attention?

"If my record's coming out but people are interested in your other stuff more than they are that. So we're just kind of doing our thing, we're working right now".

Lisa did want to keep on singing, though?

"Yes, I do".

Presley would keep on writing?

"As long as I know that what I'm doing is helping others, or contributing to something good, I'll continue".

Was Lisa Marie happy?

"Yes. Very happy".

Happiest ever?

"Yes, without a doubt".

Because of her career, Michael, the whole ball of wax, Riley, mum".

"All of it, everything is in order right this minute, everything. All the ducks are in a row, quacking in the same direction right now, and it seems that's great. I hate saying that kind of stuff, because then you think about it, you're like, 'Ah, what's going to happen?'".

Didn't want to jinx it. Folk got mad, because they didn't like to see Lisa happy.

"Of course they don't. A majority -- at least 20% of the population doesn't".

That's a lot.

"It is, actually, when you think about it".

Did Presley worry about what people thought about her?

"It'd affect me. I'm greatly affected when I feel negativity, particularly. It does definitely have its effect".

Who didn't want to be liked?

"Right. To some degree, you do. I mean, you can put up as much of a front as you want, but the bottom line is that everyone's affected by somebody wanting to take them down'.

Continued good luck, doll.

"Thank you very much, Sir".

68

Michael Joseph Jackson, born in Gary, Chicago, Indiana, on August 29, 1958, was an American singer, songwriter and dancer. Known as the "King of Pop", he was one of the most popular entertainers in the world, being the best-selling music artist at the time of his death. Jackson's contributions to music, dance, and fashion, along with his highly publicized personal life, made him a globally significant figure in popular culture for over four decades.

The eighth child of the Jackson family, Michael made his professional debut in 1964, with his elder brothers Jackie, Tito, Jermaine, and Marlon, as a member of the Jackson 5. He began his solo career in 1971, with Motown Records. In the early 1980s, Jackson became the leading figure in popular music.

His music videos, including those of "Beat It", "Billie Jean", and "Thriller" from his 1982 album Thriller, were credited with breaking racial barriers and transforming the medium into an art form and promotional tool, their popularity helping bring the television channel MTV to fame. Jackson's 1987 album Bad spawned the U.S. Billboard Hot 100 number-one singles "I Just Can't Stop Loving You", "Bad", "The Way You Make Me Feel", "Man in the Mirror", and "Dirty Diana", becoming the first album to have five number-one singles in the US.

He continued to innovate with videos such as "Black or White" and "Scream" during the 1990s, developing his reputation as a touring solo artist. Through stage and video performances, Jackson popularized a number of complicated dance techniques, such as the robot and the moonwalk. His distinctive sound and style influenced numerous artists in various music genres.

Thriller was the best-selling album of all time, with estimated sales of 65 million copies worldwide. Jackson's other albums, including Off the Wall (1979), Bad (1987), Dangerous (1991), and HIStory (1995), also rank among the world's best-selling albums. He is one of the few artists to have been inducted into the Rock and Roll Hall of Fame twice, also being inducted into the Songwriters Hall of Fame and the Dance Hall of Fame, the only dancer from pop and rock music.

He holds multiple Guinness World Records including the Most Successful Entertainer of All Time, 13 Grammy Awards, the Grammy Legend Award, the Grammy Lifetime Achievement Award, 26 American Music Awards—more than any other artist—including the "Artist of the Century" and "Artist of the 1980s", 13 number-one singles in the United States during his solo career—more than any other male artist in the Hot 100 era—with estimated sales of over 350 million records worldwide.

Jackson won hundreds of awards, making him the most awarded recording artist in the history of popular music. He became the first artist in history to have a top ten single in the Billboard Hot 100 in five different decades when "Love Never Felt So Good" reached number nine on May 21, 2014. Jackson traveled the world attending events honouring his humanitarianism, and, in 2000, the Guinness World Records recognized him for supporting 39 charities, more than any other entertainer.

Aspects of Jackson's personal life were controversial, including his changing appearance, personal relationships, and his behavior. In 1993, he was accused of child sexual abuse, but the civil case was settled out of court for an undisclosed amount, no formal charges being brought. In 2005, he was tried and acquitted of further child sexual abuse allegations, with several other charges, after the jury found him not guilty on all counts.

While preparing for his comeback concert series, This Is It, Jackson died of acute propofol and benzodiazepine intoxication on June 25, 2009, suffering a cardiac arrest. The Los Angeles County Coroner ruled his death a homicide, his personal physician, Conrad Murray, being convicted of involuntary manslaughter. Jackson's death triggered a global outpouring of grief, a live broadcast of his public memorial service being viewed around the world.

Forbes ranked Jackson the top-earning dead celebrity, with earnings of $825 million in 2016, the highest yearly amount ever recorded by the publication. He's remembered for his philanthropy and charitable fundraising within the entertainment industry.

Michael Joseph Jackson was the eighth of ten children in the Jackson family, a working-class African-American family living in a two-bedroom house on Jackson Street in Gary, Indiana, an industrial city in the Chicago metropolitan area. His mother, Katherine Esther Scruse, was a devout Jehovah's Witness. She played clarinet and piano, an aspiring country-and-western performer, working part-time at Sears to help support the family.

Michael's father, Joseph Walter "Joe" Jackson, a former boxer, was a steelworker at U.S. Steel. Joe performed on guitar with a local rhythm and blues band, the Falcons, supplementing the family's income. Michael had three sisters, Rebbie, La Toya, and Janet, with five brothers, Jackie, Tito, Jermaine, Marlon, and Randy. A sixth brother, Marlon's twin Brandon, died shortly after birth.

Michael Jackson had a troubled relationship with his father, In 2003, Joe acknowledging that he regularly whipped him as a boy. Joe was also said to have verbally abused his son, often saying that he had a "fat nose". Jackson stated that he was physically and emotionally abused during incessant rehearsals, though he credited his father's strict discipline with playing a large part in his success.

In an interview with Martin Bashir for the 2003 documentary 'Living with Michael Jackson', Michael recalled that Joe often sat in a chair with a belt in his hand, as he and his siblings rehearsed, and that "if you didn't do it the right way, he would tear you up, really get you." Jackson's parents disputed the longstanding allegations of abuse, with Katherine stating that while whipping is considered abuse today, it was a common way to discipline children at the time.

Jackie, Tito, Jermaine and Marlon have also said that their father was not abusive and that the whippings, which were harder on Michael because he was younger, kept them disciplined and out of trouble. Speaking openly about his childhood in an interview with Oprah Winfrey, broadcast in February 1993, Jackson said that his youth had been lonely and isolating. His deep dissatisfaction with his appearance, his nightmares and chronic sleep problems, his tendency to remain hyper-compliant, especially with his father, and to remain childlike in adulthood, were consistent with the effects of the maltreatment he endured as a child.

In 1964, Michael and Marlon joined the Jackson Brothers—a band formed by their father, which included brothers Jackie, Tito, and Jermaine—as backup musicians playing congas and tambourine. In 1965, Michael began sharing lead vocals with his older brother Jermaine, and the group's name was changed to the Jackson 5.

The following year, the group won a major local talent show, with Jackson performing the dance to Robert Parker's 1965 hit "Barefootin'". From 1966 to 1968 they toured the Midwest, frequently performing at a string of black clubs, known as the "chitlin' circuit," as the opening act for artists such as Sam & Dave, the O'Jays, Gladys Knight, and Etta James.

The Jackson 5 also performed at clubs and cocktail lounges, where striptease shows and other adult acts were featured, and at local auditoriums and high school dances. In August 1967, while touring the East coast, the group won a weekly amateur night concert at the Apollo Theater in Harlem.

The Jackson 5 recorded several songs, including their first single "Big Boy" (1968), for Steeltown Records, a Gary record label, before signing with Motown in 1969, leaving Gary, relocating to Los Angeles, where they continued to record music for Motown. Rolling Stone later described the young Michael as "a prodigy," with "overwhelming musical gifts," who "quickly emerged as the main draw and lead singer."

The group set a chart record when its first four singles—"I Want You Back" (1969), "ABC" (1970), "The Love You Save" (1970), and "I'll Be There" (1970)—peaked at number one on the Billboard Hot 100. In May 1971, the Jackson family moved into a large home on a two-acre estate in Encino, California.

During this period, Michael evolved from child performer into a teen idol. As he began to emerge as a solo performer in the early 1970s, he maintained ties to the Jackson 5 and Motown. Between 1972 and 1975, Michael released four solo studio albums with Motown: Got to Be There (1972), Ben (1972), Music & Me (1973), and Forever, Michael (1975). "Got to Be There" and "Ben", the title tracks from his first two solo albums, became successful singles, as did a cover of Bobby Day's "Rockin' Robin".

The Jackson 5 were later described as, "a cutting-edge example of black crossover artists." Although the group's sales began to decline in 1973, with the members unhappy with Motown's refusal to allow them creative input, they achieved several top 40 hits, including the top five single "Dancing Machine" (1974), before leaving Motown in 1975.

In June 1975, the Jackson 5 signed with Epic Records, a subsidiary of CBS Records, renaming themselves 'the Jacksons'. Younger brother Randy formally joined the band around this time, while Jermaine chose to stay with Motown to pursue a solo career. The Jacksons continued to tour internationally, releasing six more albums between 1976 and 1984. Michael, the group's lead songwriter during this time, wrote hits such as "Shake Your Body (Down to the Ground)" (1979), "This Place Hotel" (1980), and "Can You Feel It" (1980).

Michael Jackson's film work in began in 1978, when he moved to New York City to star as the Scarecrow in The Wiz, a musical directed by Sidney Lumet. It co-starred Diana Ross, Nipsey Russell, and Ted Ross but he film was a box-office failure. Its score was arranged by Quincy Jones, whom Jackson had previously met when he was 12, at Sammy Davis Jr.'s house. Jones agreed to produce Jackson's next solo album.

During his time in New York, Jackson frequented the Studio 54 nightclub, being exposed to early hip hop, influencing his beatboxing on future tracks, such as "Working Day and Night". In 1979, Jackson broke his nose during a complex dance routine, his subsequent rhinoplasty not being a complete success. As he complained of breathing difficulties that would affect his career, he was referred to Dr. Steven Hoefflin, who performed Jackson's second rhinoplasty and subsequent operations.

Jackson's fifth solo album, Off the Wall (1979), co-produced by Michael and Jones, established Jackson as a solo performer. The album helped Michael transition from the bubblegum pop of his youth, to the more complex sounds he would create as an adult. Songwriters for the album included Michael Jackson, Rod Temperton, Stevie Wonder, and Paul McCartney.

Off the Wall was the first solo album to generate four top 10 hits in the United States: "Off the Wall", "She's Out of My Life", and the chart-topping singles "Don't Stop 'Til You Get Enough" and "Rock with You". The album reached number three on the Billboard 200, eventually selling over 20 million copies worldwide.

In 1980, Jackson won three gongs at the American Music Awards for his solo efforts: Favorite Soul/R&B Album, Favorite Soul/R&B Male Artist, and Favorite Soul/R&B Single for "Don't Stop 'Til You Get Enough". He also won Billboard Year-End awards for Top Black Artist and Top Black Album, and a Grammy Award for Best Male R&B Vocal Performance for 1979, with "Don't Stop 'Til You Get Enough".

In 1981 Jackson was the American Music Awards winner for Favorite Soul/R&B Album and Favorite Soul/R&B Male Artist. Despite its commercial success, Jackson felt Off the Wall should have made a bigger impact, being determined to exceed expectations with his next release. In 1980, he secured the highest royalty rate in the music industry: 37 percent of wholesale album profit.

Jackson recorded with Queen vocalist Freddie Mercury from 1981 to 1983, including a demo of "State of Shock", "Victory" and "There Must Be More to Life Than This". The recordings were intended for an album of duets but Queen's then-manager Jim Beach, said the relationship between the singers soured, when Jackson insisted on bringing a llama into the recording studio, so the collaborations were not officially released until 2014.

Jackson went on to record the single "State of Shock" with Mick Jagger, for the Jacksons' album Victory (1984). Mercury included the solo version of "There Must Be More To Life Than This," on his Mr. Bad Guy album (1985). In 1982, Jackson combined his interests in songwriting and film, when he contributed the song "Someone in the Dark," to the storybook for the film E.T. the Extra-Terrestrial. The song, with Jones as its producer, won a Grammy for Best Recording for Children, 1983.

Massive success came with Jackson's sixth album, Thriller, released in late 1982. The album earned Jackson seven more Grammys and eight American Music Awards, including the Award of Merit, the youngest artist to win it. It was the best-selling album worldwide in 1983, becoming both the best-selling album of all time in the United States and the best-selling album of all time worldwide, selling an estimated 65 million copies.

It topped the Billboard 200 chart for 37 weeks, remaining in the top 10 of the 200 for 80 consecutive weeks. It was the first album to have seven Billboard Hot 100 top 10 singles, including "Billie Jean", "Beat It", and "Wanna Be Startin' Somethin'". In December 2015, Thriller was certified for 30 million shipments by the RIAA, making it the only album to achieve that feat in the United States.

Thriller won Michael Jackson and Quincy Jones, the Grammy award for Producer of the Year (Non-Classical) for 1983. It also won Album of the Year, with Jackson as the album's artist and Jones as its co-producer, and a Best Pop Vocal Performance, Male, award for Jackson. "Beat It" won Record of the Year, with Jackson as artist and Jones as co-producer, and a Best Rock Vocal Performance, Male, award for Jackson.

"Billie Jean" won Jackson two Grammy awards, Best R&B Song, with Jackson as its songwriter, and Best R&B Vocal Performance, Male, as its artist. Thriller also won another Grammy for Best Engineered Recording – Non Classical in 1984, awarding Bruce Swedien for his work on the album. The AMA Awards for 1984 provided Jackson with an Award of Merit and AMAs for Favorite Male Artist, Soul/R&B, and Favorite Male Artist, Pop/Rock. "Beat It" won Jackson AMAs for Favorite Video, Soul/R&B, Favorite Video, Pop/Rock, and Favorite Single, Pop/Rock. Thriller won him AMAs for Favorite Album, Soul/R&B, and Favorite Album, Pop/Rock.

In addition to the album, Jackson released "Thriller", a 14-minute music video directed by John Landis, in 1983. The zombie-themed video, "defined music videos and broke racial barriers" on the Music Television Channel (MTV), a fledgling entertainment television channel at the time. Jackson had the highest royalty rate in the music industry at that point, approximately $2 for every album sold, making record-breaking profits from sales of his recordings.

The videocassette of the documentary The Making of Michael Jackson's Thriller, sold over 350,000 copies in a few months. The era saw the arrival of novelties such as dolls modeled after Jackson, which appeared in stores in May 1984 at a price of $12. Biographer J. Randy Taraborrelli wrote that "Thriller stopped selling like a leisure item—like a magazine, a toy, tickets to a hit movie—and started selling like a household staple."

In December 2009, the Library of Congress selected the "Thriller" music video for inclusion in the National Film Registry, it being one of 25 films named that year as "works of enduring importance to American culture" that would be "preserved for all time," the only music video to have been inducted into the registry.

In 1985, The Making of Michael Jackson's Thriller won a Grammy for Best Music Video, Longform. Time described Jackson's influence at that point as "star of records, radio, rock video, a one-man rescue team for the music business. A songwriter who sets the beat for a decade. A dancer with the fanciest feet on the street. A singer who cuts across all boundaries of taste and style and colour too". The New York Times wrote that "in the world of pop music, there is Michael Jackson and there is everybody else".

On March 25, 1983, Michael Jackson reunited with his brothers for a performance taped at the Pasadena Civic Auditorium for Motown 25: Yesterday, Today, Forever, an NBC television special. The show aired on May 16, 1983, to an estimated audience of 47 million, featuring the Jacksons and other Motown stars.

It is best remembered for Michael Jackson's solo performance of "Billie Jean", which earned him his first Emmy nomination. Wearing a distinctive black-sequined jacket and a golf glove, decorated with rhinestones, he debuted his signature dance move, the 'moonwalk', which former Soul Train dancer and Shalamar member, Jeffrey Daniel, had taught him three years earlier.

Jackson had originally turned down the invitation to perform at the show, believing he had been doing too much television at the time but at the request of Motown founder Berry Gordy, he agreed to perform, in exchange for the solo performance time. Rolling Stone reporter Mikal Gilmore said, "There are times when you know you are hearing or seeing something extraordinary ... that came that night." Jackson's performance drew comparisons to Elvis Presley's and the Beatles' appearances on The Ed Sullivan Show.

Anna Kisselgoff of The New York Times wrote in 1988: "The moonwalk that he made famous is an apt metaphor for his dance style. How does he do it? As a technician, he is a great illusionist, a genuine mime. His ability to keep one leg straight as he glides, while the other bends and seems to walk, requires perfect timing." Gordy said of the performance: "From the first beat of 'Billie Jean', I was mesmerized, and when he did his iconic moonwalk, I was shocked, it was magic, Michael Jackson went into orbit, and never came down".

In November 1983 Michael Jackson and his brothers partnered with PepsiCo, in a $5 million promotional deal that broke records for a celebrity endorsement. The first Pepsi Cola campaign, which ran in the United States from 1983 to 1984, launching its iconic "New Generation" theme, included tour sponsorship, public relations events, and in-store displays.

Michael Jackson, who was involved in creating the advertisement, suggested using his song "Billie Jean" as its jingle, with revised lyrics. According to a Billboard report in 2009, Brian J. Murphy, executive VP of branded management at TBA Global, said: "You couldn't separate the tour, from the endorsement, from the licensing of the music, and then the integration of the music into the Pepsi fabric."

On January 27, 1984, Michael and other members of the Jacksons filmed a Pepsi commercial overseen by executive Phil Dusenberry, a BBDO ad agency executive, and Alan Pottasch, Pepsi's Worldwide Creative Director, at the Shrine Auditorium in Los Angeles. During a simulated concert, before a full house of fans, pyrotechnics accidentally set Jackson's hair on fire, causing second-degree burns to his scalp.

Michael underwent treatment to hide the scars, having his third rhinoplasty shortly thereafter. Pepsi settled out of court, Jackson donating the $1.5 million settlement to the Brotman Medical Center in Culver City, California; its Michael Jackson Burn Center was named in his honour. Dusenberry recounted the episode in his memoir, Then We Set His Hair on Fire: Insights and Accidents from a Hall of Fame Career in Advertising.

Jackson signed a second agreement with Pepsi in the late 1980s, for a reported $10 million. The second campaign had a global reach of more than 20 countries, providing financial support for Michael's Bad album and 1987–88 world tour. Although Jackson had endorsements and advertising deals with other companies, such as LA Gear, Suzuki, and Sony, none were as significant as his deals with Pepsi, which later signed other music stars such as Britney Spears and Beyoncé to promote its products.

Jackson's humanitarian work was recognized on May 14, 1984, when he was invited to the White House to receive an award from President Ronald Reagan, for his support of charities that helped people overcome alcohol and drug abuse, and in recognition of his support for the Ad Council's and the National Highway Traffic Safety Administration's Drunk Driving Prevention campaign. Jackson donated the use of "Beat It," for the campaign's public service announcements.

Unlike later albums, Thriller did not have an official tour, but the Victory Tour of 1984 headlined the Jacksons, showcasing much of Jackson's new solo material to more than two million Americans, the last time he was to tour with his brothers. Following controversy over the concert's ticket sales, Jackson held a press conference, announcing that he would donate his share of the proceeds, an estimated $3 to 5 million, to charity.

His charitable work and humanitarian awards continued, with the release of "We Are the World" (1985), co-written with Lionel Richie. The song was recorded on January 28, 1985, being released worldwide in March 1985, to aid the poor in the United States and Africa. The song earned $63 million for famine relief, becoming one of the best-selling singles of all time, with 20 million copies sold.

It won four 1985 Grammys, including Song of the Year for Jackson and Richie as its writers. Although the American Music Award directors removed the charity song from the competition, because they felt it would be inappropriate, the AMA show in 1986 concluded with a tribute to the song, in honour of its first anniversary. The project's creators received two special AMA honors: one for the creation of the song and another for the USA for Africa idea. Jackson, Jones, and entertainment promoter Ken Kragan received special awards for their roles in the song's creation.

Michael Jackson's financial interests in the music publishing business grew, after he collaborated with Paul McCartney in the early 1980s, learning that McCartney was making approximately $40 million a year from other people's songs. By 1983, Jackson had begun investing in publishing rights to songs that others had written, but he was careful with his acquisitions, only bidding on a few of the dozens that were offered to him.

Michael's early acquisitions of music catalogs and song copyrights, included the Sly Stone collection, "Everyday People" (1968), Len Barry's "1-2-3" (1965), and Dion DiMucci's "The Wanderer" (1961) and "Runaround Sue" (1961). However, his most significant purchase came in 1985, when he acquired the publishing rights to ATV Music Publishing after months of negotiation. ATV had acquired the publishing rights to nearly 4000 songs, including the Northern Songs catalog that contained the majority of the Lennon–McCartney compositions recorded by the Beatles.

In 1984 Robert Holmes à Court, the wealthy Australian investor who owned ATV Music Publishing, announced he was putting the ATV catalog up for sale. In 1981, McCartney was offered the ATV music catalog for £20 million ($40 million). According to McCartney, he contacted Yoko Ono about making a joint purchase, by splitting the cost at £10 million each, but Ono thought they could buy it for £5 million each.

When they were unable to make a joint purchase, McCartney, who did not want to be the sole owner of the Beatles' songs, did not pursue an offer on his own. According to a negotiator for Holmes à Court in the 1984 sale, McCartney was given first right of refusal but declined to purchase. Michael Jackson was informed of the sale by his attorney, John Branca, in September 1984.

An attorney for McCartney also assured Branca that McCartney was not interested in bidding, believing it was too expensive, but several other companies and investors were interested in bidding. Jackson submitted a bid of $46 million on November 20, 1984, his agents thinking they had a deal several times, but encountering new bidders or new areas of debate.

In May 1985, Jackson's team left the talks, after having spent more than $1 million and four months of due diligence work on the negotiations. In June 1985, Michael and Branca learned that Charles Koppelman's and Marty Bandier's The Entertainment Company, had made a tentative agreement with Holmes à Court to buy ATV Music for $50 million; however, in early August, Holmes à Court's team contacted Jackson and talks resumed.

Michael Jackson raised his bid to $47.5 million, which was accepted because he could close the deal more quickly, having already completed due diligence of ATV Music. Jackson also agreed to visit Holmes à Court in Australia, where he would appear on the Channel Seven Perth Telethon.Jackson's purchase of ATV Music was finalized on August 10, 1985.

Jackson's skin had been a medium-brown colour during his youth, but from the mid-1980s gradually grew paler. The change gained widespread media coverage, including rumours that he might have been bleaching his skin. J. Randy Taraborrelli stated that Jackson was diagnosed with vitiligo in 1984, which results in white patches on the skin.

Michael had also been diagnosed with lupus, both illnesses making Jackson's skin sensitive to sunlight but the lupus was in remission. The treatments he used for his condition further lightened his skin, and with the application of pancake makeup to even out blotches he could appear pale.

Jackson stated that although he used makeup to control the patchy appearance of his skin, he never purposely bleached his skin. He said of his vitiligo: "It is something I cannot help. When people make up stories that I don't want to be who I am, it hurts me. It's a problem for me. I can't control it." Jackson was also diagnosed with vitiligo in his autopsy, though not lupus.

Michael said he'd had only two rhinoplasties, no other facial surgery, although at one point mentioned having had a dimple created in his chin. He lost weight in the early 1980s, because of a change in diet and a desire for "a dancer's body". Witnesses reported that he was often dizzy, speculating that he was suffering from anorexia nervosa, periods of weight loss becoming a recurring problem later in life.

During the course of his treatment, Jackson made two close friends: his dermatologist, Dr. Arnold Klein, and Klein's nurse Debbie Rowe, who eventually became Michael's second wife and the mother of his two eldest children. He also relied heavily on Klein for medical and business advice.

In 1986, the tabloids ran a story claiming that he slept in a hyperbaric oxygen chamber to slow the aging process, including pictures of him lying in a glass box. Although the claim was untrue, the tabloids later stated that Jackson disseminated the fabricated story himself. When Jackson bought a chimpanzee named Bubbles from a laboratory, he was said to be increasingly detached from reality.

It was reported that Jackson had tried to buy the bones of Joseph Merrick (the "Elephant Man"), although untrue, Michael not denying the story. Although he was believed to have initially seen these stories as opportunities for publicity, after they'd become more sensational, the apparent false leaks ceased. However, the media continued to publish fabricated stories, which became embedded in the public consciousness, inspiring the nickname "Wacko Jacko", which Jackson despised. Responding to the gossip, Jackson remarked to Taraborrelli:

Why not just tell people I'm an alien from Mars? Tell them I eat live chickens and do a voodoo dance at midnight. They'll believe anything you say, because you're a reporter but if I, Michael Jackson, were to say, "I'm an alien from Mars and I eat live chickens and do a voodoo dance at midnight," people would say, "Oh, man, that Michael Jackson is nuts. He's cracked up. You can't believe a single word that comes out of his mouth."

Jackson collaborated with filmmakers George Lucas and Francis Ford Coppola on the 17-minute 3D film Captain EO, which debuted in September 1986 at both the original Disneyland and at Epcot in Florida then in March 1987 at Tokyo Disneyland. The $30 million movie was a popular attraction at all three parks. A Captain EO attraction was later featured at Euro Disneyland, after that park opened in 1992.

All four parks' Captain EO installations stayed open well into the 1990s: the Paris installation was the last to close, in 1998. The attraction would later return to Disneyland in 2010, after Jackson's death. In 1987, Jackson disassociated himself from the Jehovah's Witnesses, in response to their disapproval of the Thriller video.

With the industry expecting another major hit, Jackson's first album in five years, Bad (1987), was highly anticipated. The album produced nine singles, with seven charting in the U.S, five of which, "I Just Can't Stop Loving You", "Bad", "The Way You Make Me Feel", "Man in the Mirror", and "Dirty Diana," reached number one on the Billboard Hot 100, a record for most number-one Hot 100 singles from any one album.

By 2012, the album had sold between 30 and 45 million copies worldwide. Bruce Swedien and Humberto Gatica won a Grammy in 1988, for Best Engineered Recording – Non Classical and Michael Jackson won a Grammy for Best Music Video, Short Form, for "Leave Me Alone" in 1989. In the same year, Jackson won an Award of Achievement at the American Music Awards, after Bad became the first album to top in 25 countries, and the best-selling album worldwide in 1987 and 1988. In 1988, "Bad" won an American Music Award for Favorite Soul/R&B Single.

The Bad World Tour began on September 12th '88, finishing on January 14, 1989. In Japan alone, the tour had 14 sellouts, drawing 570,000 people, nearly tripling the previous record of 200,000 on a single tour. Jackson broke a Guinness World Record, when 504,000 people attended seven sold-out shows at Wembley Stadium. He performed a total of 123 concerts to an audience of 4.4 million people.

In 1988, Jackson released his only autobiography, Moonwalk, which took four years to complete, selling 200,000 copies. He wrote about his childhood, the Jackson 5, the abuse he'd suffered and his changing facial appearance, attributing it to puberty, weight loss, a strict vegetarian diet, a change in hairstyle, and stage lighting. Moonwalk reached the top position on The New York Times best sellers' list.

Jackson released a film, Moonwalker, which featured live footage and short films starring Jackson and Joe Pesci. Due to financial issues, the film was only released in movie theatres in Germany, in other markets being released direct-to-video. It debuted at the top of the Billboard Top Music Video Cassette chart, staying there for 22 weeks, before being knocked off the top spot by Michael Jackson: The Legend Continues.

In March 1988, Michael purchased land near Santa Ynez, California, to build Neverland Ranch, at a cost of $17 million. He installed several carnival rides on the 2,700-acre (11 km2) property, including a Ferris wheel, carousel, menagerie, movie theatre and zoo, with a security staff of 40 patrolling the grounds. In 2003, it was valued at approximately $100 million. In 1989, Jackson's annual earnings from album sales, endorsements, and concerts were estimated at $125 million. Shortly afterwards, he became the first Westerner to appear in a television ad in the Soviet Union.

Jackson's success earned him the nickname the "King of Pop," which was popularized by Elizabeth Taylor, when she presented him with the Soul Train Heritage Award in 1989, proclaiming him "the true king of pop, rock and soul." President George H. W. Bush designated him the White House's "Artist of the Decade".

From 1985 to 1990, he donated $455,000 to the United Negro College Fund, and all profits from his single "Man in the Mirror" went to charity. Jackson's live rendition of "You Were There," at Sammy Davis Jr.'s 60th birthday celebration won Jackson a second Emmy nomination. In March 1991, Jackson renewed his contract with Sony for $65 million, a record-breaking deal at the time, displacing Neil Diamond's renewal contract with Columbia Records.

He released his eighth album, Dangerous that year,co-produced with Teddy Riley. Dangerous was certified seven times platinum in the U.S., by 2008 having sold c. 30 million copies worldwide. In the United States, the album's first single "Black or White," was its biggest hit, reaching number one on the Billboard Hot 100, remaining there for seven weeks, with similar chart performances worldwide.

The second single, "Remember the Time", spent eight weeks in the top five in the United States, peaking at number three on the Billboard Hot 100 singles chart. At the end of 1992, Dangerous was awarded the best-selling album of the year worldwide, "Black or White" being awarded best-selling single of the year worldwide at the Billboard Music Awards.

Jackson also won an award as best-selling artist of the 1980s. In 1993, he performed the song at the Soul Train Music Awards in a chair, saying he had suffered an injury in rehearsals. In the UK and other parts of Europe, "Heal the World" was the album's most successful song, selling 450,000 copies in the UK, spending five weeks at number two in 1992.

Jackson founded the Heal the World Foundation in 1992. The charity brought underprivileged children to Jackson's ranch to enjoy the property's theme park rides, sending millions of dollars around the globe to help children afflicted by war, poverty, and disease. In the same year, Jackson published his second book, Dancing the Dream, a collection of poetry, revealing a more intimate side.

While it was a commercial success, it received mostly negative reviews but In 2009, the book was republished by Doubleday, being more positively received by some critics in the wake of Jackson's death. The Dangerous World Tour began on June 27, 1992, finishing on November 11, 1993, having grossed $100 million, with Jackson having performed to 3.5 million people at 70 concerts.He sold the broadcast rights to his Dangerous world tour to HBO for $20 million, a record-breaking deal that still stood over 20 years later.

Following the illness and death of AIDS spokesperson Ryan White, Jackson helped draw public attention to HIV/AIDS. He publicly pleaded with the Clinton Administration at Bill Clinton's Inaugural Gala, to give more money to HIV/AIDS charities and research. In a high-profile visit to Africa, Jackson visited countries including Gabon and Egypt. His first stop in Gabon was greeted with an enthusiastic reception of more than 100,000 people, some of them carrying signs that read "Welcome Home Michael." On his trip to Ivory Coast, Jackson was crowned "King Sani" by a tribal chief. He thanked the dignitaries in French and English, signed official documents formalizing his kingship then sat on a golden throne, while watching ceremonial dances.

In January 1993, Jackson performed at the Super Bowl XXVII halftime show in Pasadena, California. Because of a dwindling interest during halftime in the preceding years, the NFL decided to seek big-name talent that would keep ratings high, with Jackson selected for his widespread appeal.

It was the first Super Bowl for which the half-time performance drew greater audience figures than the game itself. The performance began with Jackson catapulting onto the stage as fireworks went off behind him, followed by four songs: "Jam", "Billie Jean", "Black or White", and "Heal the World". Jackson's Dangerous album rose 90 places in the album chart after the performance.

Michael gave a 90-minute interview to Oprah Winfrey on February 10, 1993, only his second television interview since 1979. He grimaced when speaking of his childhood abuse at the hands of his father, saying he believed he had missed out on much of his childhood years, and that he often cried from loneliness.

He denied tabloid rumours that he had bought the bones of the Elephant Man, slept in a hyperbaric oxygen chamber, or bleached his skin, stating for the first time that he had vitiligo. Dangerous re-entered the album chart in the top 10, more than a year after its original release.

In February 1993, Jackson was given the "Living Legend Award" at the 35th Annual Grammy Awards in Los Angeles. "Black or White" was Grammy-nominated for best vocal performance. "Jam" gained two nominations: Best R&B Vocal Performance and Best R&B Song. The Dangerous album won a Grammy for Best Engineered – Non Classical, awarding the work of Bruce Swedien and Teddy Riley.

In the same year, Michael Jackson won three American Music Awards for Favorite Pop/Rock Album (Dangerous), Favorite Soul/R&B Single ("Remember the Time"), and was the first to win the International Artist Award of Excellence, for his global performances and humanitarian work.

He agreed to produce the soundtrack for Sega's 1994 video game Sonic the Hedgehog 3, with collaborators Brad Buxer, Bobby Brooks, Darryl Ross, Geoff Grace, Doug Grigsby, and Cirocco Jones. However, Jackson left the project before completion, so was not credited, some stating that he was dissatisfied with the Sega Genesis console's audio chip, while others suggested Sega distanced itself from Jackson, following the first allegations of child sexual abuse against him.

In the summer of 1993, Jackson was accused of child sexual abuse by a 13-year-old boy, Jordan Chandler, and his father, Evan Chandler, a dentist. The Chandler family demanded payment from Jackson, which he refused. Jordan Chandler eventually told the police that Jackson had sexually abused him.

However, Jordan's mother was adamant that there had been no wrongdoing on Jackson's part. Evan was recorded discussing his intention to pursue charges, saying, "If I go through with this, I win big-time. There's no way I lose. I will get everything I want and they will be destroyed forever..... Michael's career will be over."

Jackson used the recording to argue that he was the victim of a jealous father, whose only goal was to extort money. In January 1994, after an investigation, deputy Los Angeles County district attorney Michael J. Montagna stated that Chandler would not be charged with extortion, due to lack of cooperation from Jackson's party and its willingness to negotiate with Chandler for several weeks, among other reasons.

In August 1993, police raided Jackson's home and, according to court documents, found books and photographs in his bedroom, featuring young boys with little or no clothing. Since the books were legal to purchase and own, the jury decided not to indict Jackson. Jordan Chandler gave police a description of Jackson's intimate parts, a strip search revealing that Jordan had correctly described Jackson as having patchy-coloured buttocks, short pubic hair, and pink and brown marked testicles.

Jordan was also said to have drawn accurate pictures of a dark spot on Jackson's penis, only visible when it was lifted. Despite differing initial internal reports from prosecutors and investigators, with statements of jurors feeling that the photos did not match the description, the DA indicated his belief in a sworn affidavit that the description was accurate, as did the sheriff's photographer.

However, the investigation was said to be inconclusive, no charges being filed. Jackson described the search in an emotional public statement, proclaiming his innocence. On January 1, 1994, Jackson settled with the Chandlers out of court for $22 million. A Santa Barbara County grand jury and a Los Angeles County grand jury disbanded on May 2, 1994, without indicting Jackson.

The Chandlers stopped co-operating with the criminal investigation around July 6, 1994. The out-of-court settlement's documentation stated Jackson admitted no wrongdoing and no liability, the Chandlers and their family lawyer Larry Feldman signing it without contest. Feldman stated "nobody bought anybody's silence".

A 2004 motion filed by Jackson's defence team, asserted that Jackson was never criminally indicted by any grand jury that his settlement admitted no wrongdoing, containing no evidence of criminal misconduct. A decade after the fact, during the second round of child abuse allegations, Jackson's lawyers also filed a memo stating that the 1994 settlement was made without his consent.

A later disclosure by the FBI of investigation documents compiled over nearly 20 years, led Jackson's attorney to suggest that no evidence of molestation or sexual impropriety from Jackson toward minors existed. The Department of Children and Family Services (Los Angeles County), apparently investigated Jackson, beginning in 1993, with the Chandler allegation then again in 2003. Reports indicate that the LAPD and DCFS did not find credible evidence of abuse or sexual misconduct.

In May 1994, Jackson married Lisa Marie Presley, the daughter of Elvis and Priscilla Presley. They had met in 1975, when a seven-year-old Presley attended one of Jackson's family engagements at the MGM Grand Hotel and Casino, before reconnecting through a mutual friend. A friend of Presley's, said "their adult friendship began in November 1992 in L.A."

They stayed in contact every day over the telephone. As the child molestation accusations became public, Jackson became dependent on Presley for emotional support; she was concerned about his faltering health and addiction to drugs. Presley said: "I believed he didn't do anything wrong and that he was wrongly accused and yes, I started falling for him. I wanted to save him. I felt that I could do it." She was said to have persuaded Michael to settle the civil case out of court then go into rehabilitation to recover.

Jackson proposed to Presley over the telephone towards the fall of 1993, saying: "If I asked you to marry me, would you do it?" They married in the Dominican Republic in secrecy, denying it for nearly two months afterwards. The marriage was, in her words, "a married couple's life ... that was sexually active."

However, the tabloid media speculated that the wedding was a ploy to prop up Jackson's public image. The marriage ended less than two years later, with an amicable divorce settlement. In a 2010 interview with Oprah, Presley said that they had spent four more years after the divorce "getting back together and breaking up," until she decided to end it.

In June 1995, Jackson released the double album HIStory: Past, Present and Future, Book I. The first disc, HIStory Begins, was a 15-track greatest hits album (later reissued as Greatest Hits: HIStory, Volume I in 2001); the second disc, HIStory Continues, contained 13 original songs, with two cover versions.

The album debuted at number one on the charts, having been certified for seven million shipments in the US. It was the best-selling multiple-disc album of all-time, with 20 million copies (40 million units) sold worldwide. HIStory received a Grammy nomination for Album of the Year.

The first single released from HIStory was "Scream/Childhood". "Scream", a duet with Jackson's youngest sister Janet, protested against the media, particularly its treatment of him during the 1993 child abuse allegations. The single had the highest debut on the Billboard Hot 100 at number five, receiving a Grammy nomination for "Best Pop Collaboration with Vocals".

"You Are Not Alone" was the second single released from HIStory, holding the Guinness World Record for the first song ever to debut at number one on the Billboard Hot 100 chart. It was seen as a major artistic and commercial success, receiving a Grammy nomination for "Best Pop Vocal Performance".

In late 1995, Jackson was rushed to a hospital after collapsing during rehearsals for a televised performance, caused by a stress-related panic attack. In November, Jackson merged his ATV Music catalog with Sony's music publishing division, creating Sony/ATV Music Publishing. He retained ownership of half the company, earning $95 million up front as well as the rights to more songs.

"Earth Song" was the third single released from HIStory, topping the UK Singles Chart for six weeks over Christmas 1995, selling a million copies, making it Jackson's most successful single in the UK. The track "They Don't Care About Us" became controversial, when the Anti-Defamation League and other groups criticized its allegedly antisemitic lyrics. Jackson quickly released a revised version of the song, without the offending lyrics. In 1996, Michael won a Grammy for Best Music Video, Short Form for "Scream" and an American Music Award for Favorite Pop/Rock Male Artist.

HIStory was promoted with the successful HIStory World Tour, beginning on September 7, 1996, ending on October 15, 1997. Jackson performed 82 concerts in five continents, 35 countries and 58 cities to over 4.5 million fans, grossing $165 million, Jackson's most successful tour in terms of audience figures.

During the tour, Jackson married his longtime friend Deborah Jeanne Rowe, a dermatology nurse, in an impromptu ceremony in Sydney, Australia. Rowe was approximately six months pregnant with the couple's first child at the time. Originally, Rowe and Jackson had no plans to marry, but Jackson's mother Katherine persuaded them to do so.

Michael Joseph Jackson Jr., commonly known as Prince, was born on February 13, 1997 then his sister Paris-Michael Katherine Jackson was born a year later on April 3, 1998. The couple divorced in 1999, Jackson receiving full custody of the children. The divorce was relatively amicable, but a subsequent custody suit was not settled until 2006.

In 1997, Jackson released Blood on the Dance Floor: HIStory in the Mix, which contained remixes of hit singles from HIStory and five new songs. Worldwide sales of 6 million copies, made it the best-selling remix album of all time. It reached number one in the UK, as did the title track. In the US, the album was certified platinum, but only reached number 24. Forbes placed Jackson's annual income at $35 million in 1996 and $20 million in 1997.

From October 1997 to September 2001, Jackson worked with collaborators including Teddy Riley and Rodney Jerkins to produce what would be his tenth solo album, Invincible. The album cost $30 million to record, not including promotional expenditures. Throughout June 1999, Jackson was involved in a number of charitable events.

He joined Luciano Pavarotti for a benefit concert in Modena, Italy. The show was in support of the nonprofit organization War Child, raising a million dollars for the refugees of Kosovo, FR Yugoslavia, with additional funds for the children of Guatemala. Later that month, Jackson organized a series of "Michael Jackson & Friends" benefit concerts, in Germany and South Korea.

Other artists involved included Slash, The Scorpions, Boyz II Men, Luther Vandross, Mariah Carey, A. R. Rahman, Prabhu Deva Sundaram, Shobana, Andrea Bocelli, and Luciano Pavarotti. The proceeds went to the Nelson Mandela Children's Fund, the Red Cross and UNESCO. From August 1999 through 2000, he lived in New York City at 4 East 74th Street. At the turn of the century, Jackson won an American Music Award as Artist of the 1980s.

In September 2001, two 30th Anniversary concerts were held at Madison Square Garden to mark Jackson's 30th year as a solo artist. Jackson appeared onstage alongside his brothers for the first time since 1984. The show also featured performances by artists including Mýa, Usher, Whitney Houston, NSYNC, Destiny's Child, Monica, Luther Vandross, and Slash.

The second show took place the night before the September 11, 2001, terrorist attacks. After 9/11, Jackson helped organize the United We Stand: What More Can I Give benefit concert, at RFK Stadium in Washington, D.C. The concert took place on October 21, 2001, including performances from dozens of major artists, including Michael, who performed his song "What More Can I Give" as the finale.

Due to contractual issues related to the earlier 30th Anniversary concerts, later edited into a two-hour TV special titled Michael Jackson: 30th Anniversary Celebration, broadcast in November 2001, Jackson's solo performances were omitted from the televised benefit concert, although he could still be seen singing backing vocals.

The release of Invincible was preceded by a dispute between Jackson and his record label, Sony Music Entertainment. Michael had expected the licenses to the masters of his albums to revert to him some time in the early 2000s, after which he would be able to promote the material however he pleased, keeping the profits; however, clauses in the contract set the revert date years into the future.

Jackson discovered that the attorney who had represented him in the deal, had also been representing Sony. He was also concerned that for years Sony had been pressuring him to sell his share in its music catalog venture; he feared that Sony might have had a conflict of interest, as if Jackson's career failed, he would have had to sell his share of the catalog at a low price, so Jackson sought an early exit from his contract.

The much anticipated 'Invincible,' was released on October 30, 2001, Jackson's first full-length album in six years, the last of original material which he released in his lifetime. It debuted at number one in 13 countries, going on to sell approximately 13 million copies worldwide. It received double-platinum certification in the U.S.

However, sales for Invincible were lower than Jackson's previous releases, due in part to the record label dispute and the lack of promotion or tour, its release coming at a bad time for the music industry in general. Invincible spawned three singles, "You Rock My World", "Cry", and "Butterflies", the latter without a music video.

On January 22, 2002, Jackson won his 22nd American Music Award, for Artist of the Century. On February 22 of the same year, his third child, Prince Michael Jackson II, nicknamed "Blanket" was born. The mother's identity was not announced, but Jackson said Prince was the result of artificial insemination from a surrogate mother and his own sperm.

Michael alleged in July 2002 that the then-Sony Music chairman Tommy Mottola was a "devil" and "racist," who did not support his African-American artists, using them merely for his own gain. He accused Mottola of having called his colleague Irv Gotti a "fat nigger". Sony refused to renew Jackson's contract, claiming that a $25 million promotional campaign had failed, because Jackson refused to tour in the United States.

Beginning in May 2002, Jackson allowed a documentary film crew, led by British TV journalist Martin Bashir, to follow him around nearly everywhere he went. On November 20 of that year, Jackson brought his infant son Prince onto the balcony of his room at the Hotel Adlon in Berlin as fans stood below, holding him in his right arm with a cloth loosely draped over Prince's face.

Prince was briefly extended over a railing, four stories above ground level, prompting widespread criticism in the media. Jackson later apologized for the incident, calling it "a terrible mistake". Bashir's crew was with Jackson during this incident, the program being broadcast in March 2003 as Living with Michael Jackson. In a particularly controversial scene, Jackson was seen holding hands and discussing sleeping arrangements with a young boy.

As soon as the documentary aired, the Santa Barbara county attorney's office began a criminal investigation. After an initial probe from the LAPD and DCFS was conducted in February 2003, they had initially concluded that molestation allegations were "unfounded." After the young boy involved in the documentary and his mother had told investigators that Jackson had behaved improperly, Michael was arrested in November 2003 then charged with seven counts of child molestation and two counts of administering an intoxicating agent, in relation to the 13-year-old boy shown in the film.

Jackson denied the allegations, saying the sleepovers were not sexual in nature. The People v. Jackson trial began on January 31, 2005, in Santa Maria, California, lasting until the end of May. On June 13, 2005, Michael was acquitted on all counts. After the trial, in a highly publicized relocation, he moved to the Persian Gulf island of Bahrain, as a guest of Sheikh Abdullah. Unknown to Jackson, Bahrain was also where the family had intended to send Michael if he had been convicted, according to a statement by Jermaine Jackson printed in The Times of London in September 2011.

On November 17, 2003, three days before Jackson's arrest, Sony released Number Ones, a compilation of Jackson's hits on CD and DVD. In the U.S., the album was certified triple platinum by the RIAA; in the UK it was certified six times platinum, for shipments of at least 1.2 million units.

In March 2006, amidst reports that Jackson was having financial problems, the main house at Neverland Ranch was closed as a cost-cutting measure. Jackson had been delinquent on his repayments of a $270 million loan secured against his music-publishing holdings, even though the holdings were reportedly making him as much as $75 million a year.

Bank of America sold the debt to Fortress Investments. Sony reportedly proposed a restructuring deal, which would give them a future option to buy half of Jackson's stake in their jointly-owned publishing company, leaving Jackson with a 25% stake. Jackson agreed to a Sony-backed refinancing deal in April 2006, although the details were not made public. Jackson did not have a recording contract at the time. In early 2006, it was announced that Jackson had signed a contract with a Bahrain-based startup, Two Seas Records but nothing came of the deal, and Two Seas CEO Guy Holmes later stated that it had never been finalized.

Throughout 2006, Sony repackaged 20 singles from the 1980s and 1990s as the Michael Jackson: Visionary series, which subsequently became a box set. Most of the singles returned to the charts as a result. In September 2006, Jackson and his ex-wife Debbie Rowe, confirmed reports that they had settled their long-running child custody suit. The terms were never made public, Jackson continuing to be the custodial parent of the couple's two children.

In October 2006, Fox News entertainment reporter Roger Friedman said that Jackson had been recording at a studio in rural Westmeath, Ireland. It was not known at the time what Jackson was working on, or who had paid for the sessions, since his publicist had recently issued a statement claiming that he had left Two Seas.

In November 2006, Jackson invited an Access Hollywood camera crew into the studio in Westmeath, MSNBC stating that he was working on a new album, produced by will.i.am. Jackson performed at the World Music Awards in London on November 15, 2006, accepting a Diamond Award for selling over 100 million records. He returned to the United States after Christmas 2006, to attend James Brown's funeral in Augusta, Georgia, where he gave one of the eulogies, saying that "James Brown is my greatest inspiration."

In 2007, Jackson and Sony bought another music publishing company, Famous Music LLC, formerly owned by Viacom. This deal gave him the rights to songs by Eminem and Beck, among others. In March 2007, Jackson gave a brief interview to the Associated Press in Tokyo, where he said:

"I've been in the entertainment industry since I was 6 years old, and as Charles Dickens would say, 'It's been the best of times, the worst of times,' but I would not change my career ... While some have made deliberate attempts to hurt me, I take it in stride, because I have a loving family, a strong faith and wonderful friends and fans who have, and continue, to support me." That month, Jackson visited a U.S. Army post in Japan, Camp Zama, to greet over 3,000 U.S. troops and their families. The hosts presented Jackson with a Certificate of Appreciation.

In September 2007, Jackson was still working on his next album, but it was never completed. In 2008, Jackson and Sony released Thriller 25, to mark the 25th anniversary of the original Thriller. The album featured the previously unreleased song "For All Time", an outtake from the original sessions, as well as remixes by younger artists who had been inspired by Jackson's work.

Two remixes were released as singles with modest success: "The Girl Is Mine 2008," with will.i.am, based on an early demo version of the original song, without Paul McCartney, and "Wanna Be Startin' Somethin' 2008," with Akon. The album was a commercial success. In anticipation of Jackson's 50th birthday, Sony BMG released a series of greatest hits albums, King of Pop. Slightly different versions were released in various countries, based on polls of local fans. King of Pop reached the top 10 in most countries where it was issued, also selling well as an import in other countries, including the United States.

In late 2008, Fortress Investments threatened to foreclose on Neverland Ranch, which Jackson used as collateral for loans running into many tens of millions of dollars. However, Fortress opted to sell Jackson's debts to Colony Capital LLC. In November, Jackson transferred Neverland Ranch's title to Sycamore Valley Ranch Company LLC, a joint venture between Jackson and Colony Capital LLC. The deal cleared Jackson's debt, being said to have earned him an additional $35 million.

At the time of his death, Jackson still owned a stake in Neverland/Sycamore Valley. In September 2008, Jackson entered negotiations with Julien's Auction House, to display and auction a large collection of memorabilia, amounting to approximately 1,390 lots. The auction was scheduled to take place between April 22 and 25. An exhibition of the lots opened as scheduled on April 14, but Jackson cancelled the auction.

In March 2009, Jackson held a press conference at London's O2 Arena, to announce a series of comeback concerts titled This Is It. The shows would have been Jackson's first major series of concerts since the HIStory World Tour finished in 1997. Jackson suggested retirement after the shows, saying it would be his "final curtain call".

The initial plan was for 10 concerts in London, followed by shows in Paris, New York City and Mumbai. Randy Phillips, president and chief executive of AEG Live, stated that the first 10 dates alone would earn the singer approximately £50 million. The London residency was increased to 50 dates, after record-breaking ticket sales, over one million having been sold in less than two hours.

The concerts would have commenced on July 13, 2009, and finished on March 6, 2010. Jackson rehearsed in Los Angeles in the weeks leading up to the tour, under the direction of choreographer Kenny Ortega. Most of these rehearsals took place at the Staples Center, owned by AEG. Less than three weeks before the first show was due to begin in London, with all concerts sold out, Jackson died after suffering cardiac arrest. Some time before his death, it was stated that he was starting a clothing line with Christian Audigier.

Jackson's first posthumous song released entirely by his estate was "This Is It", which he had co-written in the 1980s with Paul Anka. It was not on the setlists for the concerts, the recording being based on an old demo tape. The surviving brothers reunited in the studio for the first time since 1989 to record backing vocals.

On October 28, 2009, Sony released a documentary film about the rehearsals, Michael Jackson's This Is It. Despite a limited two-week engagement, it became the highest-grossing documentary or concert film of all time, with earnings of more than $260 million worldwide. Jackson's estate received 90% of the profits.

The film was accompanied by a compilation album of the same name. Two versions of "This Is It" appear on the album, which also featured original masters of Jackson's hits in the order in which they appear in the film, along with a bonus disc, with previously unreleased versions of more Jackson hits and a spoken-word poem, "Planet Earth". At the 2009 American Music Awards, Jackson won four posthumous awards, two for him and two for his album Number Ones, bringing his total American Music Awards to 26.

On June 25, 2009, Jackson stopped breathing, while attempting to sleep under the care of Conrad Murray, his personal physician. Murray had reportedly given Jackson an array of medications, in an attempt to help him sleep at his rented mansion in Holmby Hills, Los Angeles. Attempts at resuscitating Jackson were unsuccessful.

Los Angeles Fire Department paramedics received a 911 call at 12:22 pm (PDT, 19:22 UTC), arriving three minutes later. Jackson was found to not be breathing, so CPR was performed. Resuscitation efforts continued en route to Ronald Reagan UCLA Medical Center then for more than an hour after arriving there at 1:13 pm (20:13 UTC). He was pronounced dead at 2:26 pm Pacific time (21:26 UTC).

Jackson's death triggered a global outpouring of grief, the news spreading quickly online, causing websites to slow down and crash from user overload, putting unprecedented strain on websites including Google, AOL Instant Messenger, Twitter, and Wikipedia. Overall, web traffic ranged from 11% to at least 20% higher than normal.

MTV and BET aired marathons of Michael Jackson's music videos, his specials being broadcast on television stations around the world. MTV briefly returned to its original music video format, airing hours of Jackson's music videos, accompanied by live news specials, featuring reactions from MTV personalities and other celebrities.

Jackson's memorial was held on July 7, 2009 at the Staples Center in Los Angeles, preceded by a private family service at Forest Lawn Memorial Park's Hall of Liberty. Tickets to the memorial were distributed via lottery; over 1.6 million fans applied for tickets during the two-day application period. 8,750 names were drawn at random, with each recipient receiving two tickets each.

Jackson's casket was present during the memorial but no information was released about the final disposition of the body. The memorial service was one of the most watched events in streaming history, with an estimated U.S. audience of 31.1 million, comparable to the 35.1 million who watched the 2004 burial of former president Ronald Reagan and the 33.1 million Americans who watched the 1997 funeral for Princess Diana.

Mariah Carey, Stevie Wonder, Lionel Richie, John Mayer, Jennifer Hudson, Usher, Jermaine Jackson, and Shaheen Jafargholi performed at the event. Berry Gordy and Smokey Robinson gave eulogies, while Queen Latifah read "We Had Him", a poem written for the occasion by Maya Angelou.

The Reverend Al Sharpton received a standing ovation, with cheers when he told Jackson's children: "Wasn't nothing strange about your daddy. It was strange what your daddy had to deal with but he dealt with it anyway." Jackson's 11-year-old daughter Paris Katherine, speaking publicly for the first time, wept as she told the crowd: "Ever since I was born, Daddy has been the best father you could ever imagine ... I just wanted to say I love him ... so much." Reverend Lucious Smith provided a closing prayer.

At the time of death, Jackson had been administered propofol, lorazepam, and midazolam, and the Los Angeles coroner decided to treat the death as a homicide. Law enforcement officials conducted a manslaughter investigation of his personal physician Conrad Murray, charging him with involuntary manslaughter in Los Angeles, on February 8, 2010. Jackson's body was entombed on September 3, 2009, at Forest Lawn Memorial Park in Glendale, California.

On June 25, 2010, the first anniversary of Jackson's death, fans traveled to Los Angeles to pay tribute. They visited Jackson's star on the Hollywood Walk of Fame, his family home, and Forest Lawn Memorial Park. Many carried sunflowers and other tributes to leave at the sites. Members of the Jackson family and close friends arrived to pay their respects. His mother, Katherine returned to Gary, Indiana to unveil a granite monument constructed in the front yard of the family home. The memorial continued with a candlelight vigil and a special performance of "We Are the World".

On June 26, fans marched in front of the Los Angeles Police Department's Robbery-Homicide Division at the old Parker Center building, assembling a petition with thousands of signatures, demanding justice in the homicide investigation. The Jackson Family Foundation, in conjunction with Voiceplate, presented "Forever Michael", an event bringing together Jackson family members, celebrities, fans, supporters and the community to celebrate and honour his legacy, part of the proceeds being presented to some of Jackson's favorite charities.

In the 12 months after his death, Jackson sold more than 8.2 million albums in the United States and 35 million albums worldwide, making him the best-selling albums artist of 2009. He became the first artist to sell one million downloads in a week, with a record-breaking 2.6 million downloads of his songs. Three of his albums, Thriller, Number Ones and The Essential Michael Jackson, sold more than any new album, the first time a catalog album had ever had more sales than any new album.

Jackson also became the first artist in history, to have four of the top 20 best-selling albums in a single year in the United States. Following this surge in sales, Sony extended its distribution rights for Jackson's material, which had been due to expire in 2015. On March 16, 2010, Sony Music Entertainment, spearheaded by its Columbia/Epic Label Group division, signed a new deal with the Jackson estate, to extend their distribution rights to his back catalogue until at least 2017, and release ten new albums of previously unreleased material and new collections of released work.

On November 4, 2010, Sony announced the first posthumous album, Michael, released on December 14, with the promotional single, "Breaking News", released to radio on November 8. Sony Music paid the Jackson estate $250 million for the deal, plus royalties, making it the most expensive music contract pertaining to a single artist in history.

Video game developer Ubisoft announced a dancing-and-singing game featuring Michael Jackson, for the 2010 holiday season, Michael Jackson: The Experience, which was among the first games to use Kinect and PlayStation Move, the motion-detecting camera systems for Microsoft's Xbox 360 and Sony's PlayStation 3 respectively.

On November 3, 2010, the theatre company Cirque du Soleil announced that it would launch Michael Jackson: The Immortal World Tour in October 2011 in Montreal, while a permanent show would reside in Las Vegas. The 90-minute $57-million production, combined Jackson's music and choreography with the Cirque's artistry, dance and aerial displays, involving 65 artists.

On October 3, 2011, a compilation soundtrack album accompanying the tour, Immortal, was announced. A second, larger and more theatrical Cirque show, Michael Jackson: One, designed for residency at the Mandalay Bay resort in Las Vegas, was announced on February 21, 2013. The show began its run on May 23, 2013, in a newly renovated theatre, to critical and commercial success.

In April 2011, billionaire businessman Mohamed Al-Fayed, chairman of Fulham Football Club, unveiled a statue of Michael Jackson outside the club's stadium, Craven Cottage. Fulham fans were bemused by the statue, failing to understand the relevance of Jackson to the club. Al-Fayed defended the statue, telling the fans they could "go to hell" if they did not appreciate it. In September 2013 the statue was removed, being placed in the National Football Museum in Manchester in May 2014.

In 2012, in an attempt to end public family feuding, Jackson's brother Jermaine Jackson retracted his signature on a public letter, criticizing executors of Michael Jackson's estate and his mother's advisers, concerning the legitimacy of his brother's will. T.J. Jackson, son of Tito Jackson, was given co-guardianship of Michael Jackson's children, after false reports surfaced of Katherine Jackson going missing.

On May 16, 2013, choreographer Wade Robson alleged on The Today Show that Jackson "performed sexual acts on me and forced me to perform sexual acts on him" for 7 years, beginning when Robson was 7 years old. Robson had previously testified in defence of Jackson at the singer's 2005 child molestation trial. The attorney for Michael's estate described Robson's claim as "outrageous and pathetic".

The date for the hearing which would determine whether Robson could sue Jackson's estate was scheduled for June 2, 2014. In February 2014, the Internal Revenue Service reported that Michael's estate owed $702 million, including $505 million in taxes, plus $197 million in penalties, after the estate had undervalued Jackson's fortune.

On March 31, 2014, Epic Records announced Xscape, an album of eight songs of unreleased material, which was released on May 13, 2014. On May 12, 2014, another man, Jimmy Safechuck, sued Jackson's estate, claiming Jackson sexually abused him "from the age of 10 to about 14 or 15" in the 1980s.

During the 2014 Billboard Music Awards on May 18, a "Pepper's ghost" likeness of Jackson appeared, dancing to "Slave to the Rhythm", one of the tracks from Xscape. Later that year, Queen released three duets that Freddie Mercury had recorded with Jackson in the 1980s.

Jackson's earnings have exponentially increased following his death. According to Forbes, he has been the top-earning dead celebrity each year since his death, with triple-digit millions per annum ($825 million in 2016). In December 2015, Thriller became the first album in the United States to surpass 30 million shipments, certifying it 30× platinum. One year later, the album was certified again at 33× platinum, surpassing 33 million shipments, after Soundscan added streams and audio downloads to album certifications.

Jackson was influenced by musicians & other artists including Little Richard, James Brown, Jackie Wilson, Diana Ross, Fred Astaire, Sammy Davis Jr., Gene Kelly, David Ruffin,.the Isley Brothers, and the Bee Gees. While Little Richard had a substantial influence on Jackson, James Brown was his greatest inspiration; he said:

"Ever since I was a small child, no more than like six years old, my mother would wake me, no matter what time it was, if I was sleeping, no matter what I was doing, to watch the television to see the master at work and when I saw him move, I was mesmerized. I had never seen a performer perform like James Brown, and right then and there, I knew that was exactly what I wanted to do for the rest of my life, because of James Brown."

Jackson owed his vocal technique in large part to Diana Ross, especially his use of the oooh interjection, which he used from a young age; Ross had used this effect on many of the songs recorded with the

Supremes. Not only a mother figure to him, she was often observed in rehearsal as an accomplished performer.

He said: "I got to know her well. She taught me so much. I used to just sit in the corner and watch the way she moved. She was art in motion. I studied the way she moved, the way she sang – just the way she was." He told her: "I want to be just like you, Diana." She said: "You just be yourself."

Choreographer David Winters, who met and befriended Michael while choreographing the 1971 Diana Ross TV special Diana!, said Jackson watched the musical West Side Story almost every week, it being his favorite film, to which he paid tribute in "Beat It" and the "Bad" video.

Jackson explored a variety of music genres, including pop, soul, rhythm and blues, funk, rock, disco, post-disco, dance-pop and new jack swing. Unlike many artists, Jackson did not write his songs on paper, instead dictating into a sound recorder. When composing music, he preferred to beatbox and imitate instruments vocally, rather than use instruments.

According to Steve Huey of AllMusic, Thriller refined the strengths of Off the Wall; the dance and rock tracks were more aggressive, while the pop tunes and ballads were softer and more soulful. Its tracks included the ballads "The Lady in My Life", "Human Nature", and "The Girl Is Mine", the funk pieces "Billie Jean" and "Wanna Be Startin' Somethin'", Keith the disco set "Baby Be Mine" and "P.Y.T. (Pretty Young Thing)".

With Thriller, Christopher Connelly of Rolling Stone commented that Jackson developed his long association with the subliminal theme of paranoia and darker imagery. AllMusic's Stephen Thomas Erlewine noted this was evident on the songs "Billie Jean" and "Wanna Be Startin' Somethin'". In "Billie Jean", Jackson sang about an obsessive fan, who alleged that he had fathered a child of hers.

In "Wanna Be Startin' Somethin,'" he argued against gossip and the media. "Beat It" decried gang violence, in an homage to West Side Story, being Michael's first successful rock cross-over piece, saïd Huey. He also observed that the title track "Thriller" began Jackson's interest in the theme of the supernatural, a topic he revisited in subsequent years. In 1985, Michael co-wrote the charity anthem "We Are the World," humanitarian themes later becoming a recurring theme in his lyrics and public persona.

Jackson's song "Thriller", released as a single in 1984, used cinematic sound effects, horror film motifs, and vocal trickery to convey a sense of danger. A single from the album Bad, released in 1988, "Smooth Criminal" featured digital drum sounds, keyboard-created bass lines, and other percussion elements designed to give the impression of a pulsing heart. The lead single from Dangerous, "Black or White" was a danceable rock song, with hard rock elements. It was one of Michael's most successful recordings.

In the album 'Bad', Jackson's concept of the predatory lover could be seen on the rock song "Dirty Diana". The lead single "I Just Can't Stop Loving You," was a traditional love ballad, while "Man in the Mirror" was an anthemic ballad of confession and resolution. "Smooth Criminal" was an evocation of bloody assault, rape and likely murder.

AllMusic's Stephen Thomas Erlewine stated that his album, 'Dangerous,' presented Jackson as a paradoxical individual. He commented that the album was more diverse than his previous Bad, as it appealed to an urban audience, while also attracting the middle class with anthems like "Heal the World".

The first half of the record was dedicated to new jack swing, including songs like "Jam" and "Remember the Time". It was the first Jackson album in which social ills became a primary theme; "Why You Wanna Trip on Me", protesting world hunger, AIDS, homelessness and drugs. Dangerous contained sexually charged songs, such as the multifaceted love song "In the Closet".

The title track continued the theme of the predatory lover and compulsive desire. The second half included introspective, pop-gospel anthems such as "Will You Be There", "Heal the World" and "Keep the Faith," these songs showing Jackson opening up about various personal struggles and worries. In the ballad "Gone Too Soon", Michael gavé tribute to his friend Ryan White and the plight of those with AIDS.

HIStory created an atmosphere of paranoia, its content focusing on the hardships and public struggles Jackson went through prior to its production. In the new jack swing-funk-rock tracks "Scream" and "Tabloid Junkie", and the R&B ballad "You Are Not Alone", Michael retaliated against the injustice and isolation he felt, directing much of his anger at the media.

In the introspective ballad "Stranger in Moscow", Jackson lamented over his "fall from grace", while songs like "Earth Song", "Childhood", "Little Susie" and "Smile" were operatic pop pieces. In the track "D.S.", Michael launched a verbal attack against the lawyer Tom Sneddon, who had prosecuted him in both child sexual abuse cases. He describes Sneddon as an antisocial white supremacist, who wanted to "get my ass, dead or alive".

Of the song, Sneddon said: "I have not—shall we say—done him the honour of listening to it, but I've been told that it ends with the sound of a gunshot." 'Invincible,' found Jackson working heavily with producer Rodney Jerkins. The album comprised urban soul tracks such as "Cry" and "The Lost Children", ballads such as "Speechless", "Break of Dawn", and "Butterflies", mixing hip hop, pop, and R&B in "2000 Watts", "Heartbreaker" and "Invincible".

Jackson sang from childhood, over time his voice and vocal style changing noticeably. Between 1971 and 1975, his voice descended from boy soprano to high tenor. His vocal range as an adult was F2-E♭6. Michael first used the "vocal hiccup" technique, similar to gulping for air or gasping, in 1973, with the song "It's Too Late to Change the Time," from the Jackson 5's album G.I.T.: Get It Together.

Jackson did not use the technique fully until the recording of Off the Wall, when it coule be seen in full force in the "Shake Your Body (Down to the Ground)" promotional video. With the arrival of Off the Wall in the late 1970s, Michael's abilities as a vocalist were well regarded. At the time, Rolling Stone compared his vocals to the "breathless, dreamy stutter" of Stevie Wonder, writing that "Jackson's feathery-timbred tenor is extraordinarily beautiful. It slides smoothly into a startling falsetto that's used very daringly." 1982 saw the release of Thriller, when Rolling Stone was of the opinion that Jackson was then singing in a "fully adult voice" that was "tinged by sadness".

A distinctive, deliberate mispronunciation of "come on", used frequently by Jackson, occasionally spelled "c'mon", "cha'monie", or "shamone", was also a staple in impressions and caricatures of him. The turn of the 1990s saw the release of the introspective album Dangerous. The New York Times observing that on some tracks, "he gulps for breath, his voice quivers with anxiety or drops to a desperate whisper, hissing through clenched teeth" and he had a "wretched tone".

When singing of brotherhood or self-esteem, he would return to "smooth" vocals. Of Invincible, Rolling Stone was of the opinion that, at age 43, Jackson still performed "exquisitely voiced rhythm tracks and vibrating vocal harmonies". Nelson George wrote: "The grace, the aggression, the growling, the natural boyishness, the falsetto, the smoothness—that combination of elements mark him as a major vocalist".

Cultural critic Joseph Vogel wrote that Jackson had "distinctive styles is his ability to convey emotion, without the use of language: there are his trademark gulps, grunts, gasps, cries, exclamations; he also frequently scats or twists and contorts words, until they are barely discernible."

Neil McCormick stated that Michael's unorthodox singing style "was original and utterly distinctive, from his almost ethereal falsetto to his soft, sweet mid-tones; his fluid, seamless control of often very fast moving series of notes; his percussive yet still melodic outbursts, ululations and interjections (from those spooky "tee-hee-hees" to grunts and wails). Unusually for someone coming from a black American soul tradition, he did not often sing straight, unadorned ballads, though when he did,, from 'Ben' to 'She's Out of My Life', the effect was of a powerful simplicity and truth."

Jackson has been called the King of Music Videos. Steve Huey of AllMusic observed how Michael transformed the music video into an art form and a promotional tool, through complex story lines, dance routines, special effects and famous cameo appearances, simultaneously breaking down racial barriers.

Before Thriller, Jackson struggled to cet coverage on MTV, allegedly because he was African American. Pressure from CBS Records persuaded MTV to start showing "Billie Jean" then later "Beat It", leading to a lengthy partnership with Michael, also helping other black music artists gain recognition. MTV employees denied any racism in their coverage, or pressure to change their stance, maintaining that they played rock music, regardless of race.

The popularity of his videos on MTV helped to put the relatively young channel "on the map"; MTV's focus shifting in favour of pop and R&B. His performance on Motown 25: Yesterday, Today, Forever, changed the scope of live stage show; "That Jackson lip-synced 'Billie Jean' wasn't extraordinary, but that it did not change the impact of the performance was; whether the performance was live or lip-synced made no difference to the audience," thus creating an era in which artists re-created the spectacle of music video imagery on stage.

Short films like Thriller, largely remained unique to Jackson, while the group dance sequence in "Beat It" has frequently been imitated. The choreography in Thriller has become a part of global pop culture, replicated everywhere from Indian films to prisons in the Philippines. The Thriller short film marked an increase in scale for music videos, having been named the most successful music video ever made by the Guinness World Records.

In the 19-minute music video for "Bad"—directed by Martin Scorsese—Michael began using sexual imagery and choreography not previously seen in his work. He occasionally grabbed or touched his chest, torso and crotch. When asked by Oprah in the 1993 interview, about why he grabbed his crotch, he replied, "I think it happens subliminally" describing it as something that was not planned, but rather, as something that was compelled by the music.

"Bad" got a mixed reception from both fans and critics, Time magazine describing it as "infamous". The video featured Wesley Snipes; in the future Jackson's videos would often feature famous cameo roles. For the "Smooth Criminal" video, Michael experimented with an anti-gravity lean, where the performer leans forward at a 45 degree angle, beyond the performer's centre of gravity.

To accomplish this move live, Jackson and designers developed a special shoe that locked the performer's feet to the stage, allowing Jim to lean forward, Boeing granted U.S. Patent 5,255,452 for the device. Although the music video for "Leave Me Alone" was not officially released in the US, in 1989 it was nominated for three Billboard Music Video Awards, the same year winning a Golden Lion Award, for the quality of the special effects used in its production. In 1990, "Leave Me Alone" won a Grammy for Best Music Video, Short Form.

He received the MTV Video Vanguard Award in 1988 and the MTV Video Vanguard Artist of the Decade Award in 1990, to celebrate his accomplishments in the art form in the 1980s; in 1991 the first award was renamed in his honour. "Black or White" was accompanied by a controversial music video, which on November 14, 1991, simultaneously premiered in 27 countries with an estimated audience of 500 million people, the largest viewing ever for a music video at that time.

It featured scenes construed as having a sexual nature, as well as depictions of violence. The offending scenes in the final half of the 14-minute version were edited out to prevent the video from being banned, and Jackson apologized. Along with Jackson, it featured Macaulay Culkin, Peggy Lipton, and George Wendt. It helped usher in morphing, as an important technology in music videos.

"Remember the Time" was an elaborate production, Beijing one of his longest videos at over nine minutes. Set in ancient Egypt, it featured groundbreaking visual effects and appearances by Eddie Murphy, Iman, and Magic Johnson, along with a distinct complex dance routine. The video for "In the Closet," was Jackson's most sexually provocative piece, featurng supermodel Naomi Campbell in a courtship dance with Jackson. The video was banned in South Africa because of its imagery.

The music video for "Scream", directed by Mark Romanek and production designer Tom Foden, ses one of Jackson's most critically acclaimed. In 1995, it gained eleven MTV Video Music Award Nominations—more than any other music video, Winnipeg "Best Dance Video", "Best Choreography", and "Best Art Direction".

The song and its accompanying video were a response to the backlash Jackson received from the media, after being accused of child molestation in 1993. A year later, it won a Grammy for Best Music Video, Short Form; shortly afterwards Guinness World Records listed it as the most expensive music video ever made, at a cost of $7 million.

"Earth Song" was accompanied by an expensive and well-received music video, which gained a Grammy nomination for Best Music Video, Short Form in 1997. The video had an environmental theme, showing images of animal cruelty, deforestation, pollution and war. Using special effects, time was reversed, so that life returned, wars endéd, and the forests re-grew.

Released in 1997, having premiered at the 1996 Cannes Film Festival, Michael Jackson's Ghosts was a short film written by Jackson & Stephen King and directed by Stan Winston. The video for Ghosts was over 38 minutes long, holding the Guinness World Record as the world's longest music video.

The music video for "You Rock My World", which was 13 1/2 minutes long, directed by Paul Hunter, was released in 2001. The video featured appearances from Chris Tucker and Marlon Brando, winning an NAACP Image Award for Outstanding Music Video at the award shows 2002 ceremony.

The media has commonly referred to Jackson as the "King of Pop" because, throughout his career, he transformed the art of music videos, parvint the way for modern pop music. For much of Jackson's career, he had great worldwide influence over the younger generation. His music and videos, such as Thriller, fostered racial diversity in MTV's roster, steering its focus from rock to pop music and R&B, shaping the channel into a form that proved enduring. Jackson's work has continued to influence numerous artists of various music genres. He is recognized as the Most Successful Entertainer of All Time by Guinness World Records.

Danyel Smith, the chief content officer of Vibe Media Group and the editor-in-chief of Vibe, described Jackson as "The Greatest Star". AllMusic's Steve Huey Saïd Jackson was "an unstoppable juggernaut, possessed of all the skills to dominate the charts seemingly at will: an instantly identifiable voice, eye-popping dance moves, stunning musical versatility and loads of sheer star power".

BET described Jackson "as quite simply the greatest entertainer of all time," someone who "revolutionized the music video and brought dances like the moonwalk to the world. Jackson's sound, style, movement and legacy continues to inspire artists of all genres."

In 1984, Time magazine's pop critic Jay Cocks wrote that "Jackson is the biggest thing since the Beatles. He is the hottest single phenomenon since Elvis Presley. He just may be the most popular black singer ever." In 1990, Vanity Fair cited Jackson as the most popular artist in the history of show business. In 2003, Daily Telegraph writer Tom Utley described Jackson as "extremely important" and a "genius". In 2007, Jackson said: "Music has been my outlet, my gift to all of the lovers in this world. Through it, my music, I know I will live forever."

At Jackson's memorial service on July 7, 2009, Motown founder Berry Gordy proclaimed Jackson "the greatest entertainer that ever lived". In a June 28, 2009 Baltimore Sun article titled "7 Ways Michael

Jackson Changed The World", Jill Rosen wrote that Jackson's legacy was "as enduring as it is multi-faceted", influencing fields including sound, dance, fashion, music videos and celebrity. On December 19, 2014, the British Council of Cultural Relations named Jackson's life, one of the 80 most important cultural moments of the 20th century.

In July 2009, the Lunar Republic Society, which promotes the exploration, settlement, and development of the Moon, named a Moon crater after Jackson. In the same year, for Jackson's 51st birthday, Google dedicated their Google Doodle to him. In 2010, two university librarians found that Jackson's influence extended to academia, with references to Jackson in reports concerning music, popular culture, chemistry and an array of other topics.

Michael Jackson was inducted onto the Hollywood Walk of Fame in 1980, as member of the Jacksons tune in 1984 as a solo artist. Throughout his career he received numerous honours and awards, including the World Music Awards' Best-Selling Pop Male Artist of the Millennium, the American Music Award's Artist of the Century Award and the Bambi Pop Artist of the Millennium Award.

He was a double-inductee of the Rock and Roll Hall of Fame, once as a member of The Jackson 5 in 1997 then as a solo artist in 2001. Jackson was also inducted in several other halls of fame, including Vocal Group Hall of Fame, as a Jackson 5 member in 1999 and the Songwriters Hall of Fame in 2002.

In 2010, Jackson was inducted into the Dance Hall of Fame, as the first and as of '17 still thé only, dancer from the world of pop and rock 'n' roll. In 2014, Jackson was inducted into the second class of inductees to the Rhythm and Blues Music Hall of Fame; his father Joe Jackson accepted on his behalf.

His awards include many Guinness World Records, eight in 2006 alone, including for the Most Successful Entertainer of All Time, 13 Grammy Awards, the Grammy Legend Award, the Grammy Lifetime Achievement Award), 26 American Music Awards, including the "Artist of the Century" and "Artist of the 1980s",—more than any artist—13 number-one singles in the US in his solo career—more than any other male artist in the Hot 100 era—and estimated sales of over 350 million records worldwide, making him one of the best-selling artists in modern music history.

On December 29, 2009, the American Film Institute recognized Jackson's death as a "moment of significance" saying, "Michael Jackson's sudden death in June at age 50, was notable for the worldwide outpouring of grief and the unprecedented global eulogy of his posthumous concert rehearsal movie This Is It." Michael Jackson also received an Honorary Doctor of Humane Letters Degree, from the United Negro College Fund and an Honorary Doctorate of Humane Letters from Fisk University.

It is estimated that Michael Jackson earned about $750 million in his lifetime. Sales of his recordings through Sony's music unit earned him an estimated $300 million in royalties. He may have also earned an additional $400 million from concerts, music publishing, including his share of the Beatles catalog, endorsements, merchandising and music videos.

Estimating how much of these earnings Jackson was able to personally pocket is difficult, because one has to account for taxes, recording costs and production costs. There have also been several detailed estimates of Jackson's net worth during his life, which range from negative $285 million to positive $350 million, for the years 2002, 2003 and 2007.

Michael Jackson's estimated net-worth over the years

Year	Assets	Debt	Net worth	Source
2002	$130 million	$415 million	-$285 million	Forensic accountant in 2005 recalling Jackson's 2002 balance sheet under oath
2003	$550 million : $100 million in properties, including Neverland ranch; Encino and Las Vegas homes and other properties and $450 million in music holdings, including 50% stake in Sony ATV and other music publishing	$200 million	$350 million	Forbes, November 21, 2003
2007	$567.6 million : includes 50% share of the Sony/ATV catalog valued at $390.6 million, Neverland valued at $33 million, cars, antiques, collectibles and other property valued at $20 million, and $668,215 in cash	$331 million	$236 million	Michael Jackson's March 2007 statement of financial condition, prepared by Washington-based accounting firm Thompson, Cobb, Bazilio & Associates; described by CBS News as the clearest account yet of Jackson's finances.

On July 26, 2013, the executors of the Estate of Michael Jackson filed a petition in the United States Tax Court, as a result of a dispute with the Internal Revenue Service (IRS), over U.S. federal estate taxes imposed on the value of Jackson's Estate at the time of his death. The executors claimed that the Estate was worth about $7 million. The IRS asserted that the Estate was worth over $1.1 billion, and that over $700 million in federal estate taxes, including penalties, were due. A trial was held from February 6 to 24, 2017. As of early July 2017, no decision had been rendered.

In 2016, Forbes magazine estimated annual gross earnings by the Jackson Estate at $825 million, the largest ever recorded for a celebrity. The majority was due to the sale of the Sony/ATV catalog. It marked the eighth consecutive year since his death, qu'en Jackson's annual earnings were over $100 million.

Earnings after death

Year	Earnings	Source
2010	(USD 275,000,000)	

2011   (USD 170,000,000)

2012   (USD 145,000,000)

2013   (USD 160,000,000)

2014   (USD 140,000,000)

2015   (USD 115,000,000)

2016   (USD 825,000,000)

Discography

Got to Be There (1972)

Ben (1972)

Music & Me (1973)

Forever, Michael (1975)

Off the Wall (1979)

Thriller (1982)

Bad (1987)

Dangerous (1991)

HIStory: Past, Present and Future, Book I (1995)

Invincible (2001)

Filmography

The Wiz (1978)

Captain EO (1986)

Moonwalker (1988)

Michael Jackson's Ghosts (1997)

Men in Black II (2002)

Miss Cast Away and the Island Girls (2004)

Michael Jackson's This Is It (2009)

Bad 25 (2012)

Michael Jackson: The Last Photo Shoot (2014)

Michael Jackson's Journey from Motown to Off the Wall (2016)

Tours

Bad World Tour (1987–1989)

Dangerous World Tour (1992–1993)

HIStory World Tour (1996–1997)

MJ & Friends (1999)

This Is It (2009–2010; cancelled)

Printed in Great Britain
by Amazon

58531333R00059